THRILLER SHORT STORIES

Mystery, Detective, Suspense, and Psychological Fiction

This book contains 20 short stories from multiple authors.

Collected by: Morgan Black

Copyright © Morgan Black 2020

Published by VAX Books

Cover design by VAX Graphix

VaxbookZ.com

ISBN: 9798587544253

Published in the United States by VAX Graphix LLC, New York.

TABLE OF CONTENTS

Uncle Dallas

Rayhan Hidayat

It's three in the morning when the doorbell jolts Risa lucid. Another sleepless Saturday night had prompted her to grab a tub of Ben & Jerry's and drown her insomnia binging the entirety of *Black Mirror* on Netflix; she'd almost collapsed face-first onto the carpet from dehydration and enervation. She told her doctor she'd been spending most of her time completing her assignments and binge watching Netflix later on. And since she left her house on rare occasions, she was a vegetable; a cute radish preferably.

Risa skids down the stairs and looks through the peephole only to see no one waiting on the other side of the door. And when the doorbell already disrupted her sleep, she ambles to the kitchen and plucks out a coke can from the stand in the refrigerator, chugging it down.

Who could ever imagine drinking coke instead of water first thing in the morning? It was definitely Risa.

6

She reclaims her spot on the bed, cross-legged, eyes glued to the screen that has been the only light source in the room for... how many years has it been since the incident?

She hits the spacebar. A minute passes. She rewinds that minute. Another minute passes, another rewind. Not a single moment of the episode is sinking in. No matter how hard she tries, she can't peel her thoughts away from her porch, which was empty when it shouldn't have been. It gnaws at her composure, not knowing who that was. Or why anyone would visit at three in the morning.

Please be a dream, she pleads inwardly. *Please please please.*

The illusion shatters when a frantic banging noise erupts through the house and burrows through all her layers. She flinches, heart rattling in her ribcage. Her mind goes on autopilot; she wraps herself in the soothing darkness of three blankets, performs the breathing exercises her doctor taught her.

Bang bang bang.

She kicks off the sheets, gathers the dregs of courage she has remaining, and rushes downstairs. The last thing she needs is a confrontation. But she'll go crazy if the noise doesn't stop.

Risa is reverberating as much as the back door is as she readies her voice. It comes out cracked and dry from disuse, so she takes a few gulps of saliva.

7

"Whoever that is, *please stop*!"

Well, that did the trick. After a few heartbeats of stillness, a muffled voice, decidedly male, resounds from outside:

"Do not ignore me, Risa."

Risa's heart soars into a crescendo of panic. Her breaths become rapid and shallow.

"Who are you? And how do you know my name?"

The silence hangs thick in the air. Is he gone? And what did he mean by... ?

Risa heads to the front door. This mystery man must have been the one ringing the bell before growing impatient and trying to come in through the back. She checks the peephole again, in case she can catch a glimpse of her tormentor. Nothing.

She takes a deep breath. She has to do it. She unfastens all nine locks and creaks the door open. The breeze invading her nostrils is a foreign, alien scent. Holding the half-open door close like a shield, she glances across her driveway and garden; ugly and overgrown, but otherwise empty.

Empty? No, there's something on the first step of the front porch. Risa grunts as she remains in place and reaches out with a single arm; for someone like her, one step outside is setting foot in lava.

She drags the knee-high cardboard box inside and locks the door behind her.

Five minutes pulse in her ears before she regains something resembling her composure. How long has it been since someone acknowledged her existence? Or since she unlocked the door?

Risa hauls the package onto the kitchen table and stares at it, hoping that if she concentrates hard enough, she can will it out of existence, and then her life can continue on its unassuming, uneventful way. But the thought of the man returning makes her grab a boxcutter and slice it open.

Packing peanuts greet her. A piece of paper rests atop them. Her gaze tiptoes over the words scrawled on it:

My dear Risa,

Your parents may have left you, but I will always be here. As family, I fear that this lifestyle of yours does not bode well for your future. Granted, it is not always a simple matter to be coaxed out of one's shell; hence, I have prepared an impetus that should suffice. The reward for your cooperation: your overdue inheritance.

Please begin by pressing the chip to your neck, right beneath your earlobe.

Kind regards,

9

Your Uncle Dallas

A metal square the size of a thumbnail is taped below the extravagant signature. Is this the "chip" the letter mentioned? And just who is this Uncle Dallas, anyway? The last family gathering Risa remotely remembers happened an eternity ago, and there were too many faces to count, let alone recall.

She rips the chip off and does as the letter instructs. A hiss exudes her thin lips as she lines the tip of the swiss knife across the skin, making a shallow incision and inserting the chip into the flesh. Wiping off the warm blood that dribbles down her neck, Risa hauls out another letter from the box and glides through its contents that read:

Instructions to the real matter: navigate to the pink gnome in the yard where you shall get hold of another box. You are advised not to hesitate, but take it home, lest someone else discovers it. Make sure no one notices you with it.

~ Uncle Dallas

What kind of dare is this? Risa thinks to herself, baffled out of her senses. And who in the Dead Sea is this *Uncle Dallas*? He's the mastermind, the man behind the computer, drifting his fingers over the keyboard and hacking computers for hours on end. Did she ever have such a relative? As far as she knew, Java and coding puzzles never fit well with her family. They'd rather do carpentry, stitch and sing songs in a nomadic pack.

Risa steps out of her house and hugs herself as she strides toward her yard. Her legs and feet are feeble, might shatter into pieces if struck once. It's brass monkey weather today and the frosty breeze caresses her skin as it swirls through her silk red hair.

Picking up the box which is heavier than the first, she hurries inside and opens it with tentative fingers.

The air in her windpipe freezes. A pistol sits in the container like a coiled rattlesnake, as if merely touching it might lead to a grievous injury.

She's befuddled as to what's to be done with the gun. But another letter greets her from the box as she picks it up, rips off the envelope and reads the content.

I know how annoyed you must be with this sickly game. I empathize with you. But I swear this is the last letter.

You know the State Bank a few miles down the road, don't you? Get out, carry the gun and connect the dots yourself.

Sickly game? This supposed haggard, probably polishing his bald head, knows this is a game he's playing? And he empathizes?

Well, dad jokes on him!

Risa's heart is still banging hard and fierce against her chest, she's afraid of the unknown. Even though she's clueless of what's happening, she dreads the next few seconds and knows she's in peril if the task's not accomplished.

Throwing a trench coat over her shoulder and tucking away the Bryco Arm in the backpocket of her jeans, she heads out. Not even a few moments have passed since the world is exposed to her, when her eyes grow wide and transfix with horror. Anxiety thoughts are akin to driving around the block over and over, faster and faster. It's pointless.

Stop, she repeats to herself. *You're sober, so let your thoughts be as a car on a good road.*

A handful of minutes later, a huge building, the bank, comes into view and she tries suppressing her thoughts as if possessed and trying to push down the demon to the unbounded pit. It's working, at least for a little while.

Risa doesn't know how she manages to put one foot in front of the other and lock eyes with the teller. She didn't think she could leave her house, and yet here she is, on the verge of breaking a few laws along with her sanity. It's not too late to go back, maybe call the cops, she figures.

12

She flinches when a stinging pain blooms in her neck. A bystander asks if she's okay. She plays it off.

How could she forget? It's as if he's watching her every move. Well, there's no going back.

Her arm is a wet noodle as she raises the gun.

"Give... me... *money*." It takes a mountain of strength and then some to push each syllable out.

He never said how much. Not that she cares. She just wants this nightmare to be over and done with.

Things happen quickly afterwards. Panic blossoming bright and fresh in the bank as her surroundings register the threat. The teller's eyes inflating like pufferfish. A warm stream rushing down one of Risa's pant legs to pool around her shoes.

She tunes all of that out until her trench coat is stuffed with green notes.

She doesn't know how she makes it back out, but she does. In the fleeting comfort of an alleyway, she does her breathing exercises. She's about to shatter like the bottles littered at her feet.

Her phone buzzes. She stares down the text like it's about to jump out and strike her.

Enjoy your inheritance.

-Uncle D

Sirens wail in the distance. Is this some cruel, twisted joke at her expense? Divine punishment? A nightmare?

Risa darts into the lane, her hands secured around her coat pockets and hurtles away from the police car. Thanks to her athletic feet or she'd be counting days in prison. Sprinting drains her energy and as much as she wants to keep at it, she can't. She's been defeated: that's what she thinks, but a ray of hope alights in her body when a van comes forth and opens its door as if calling out to her.

The little quirk of her lips that blooms on her face feels foreign, but it's involuntary. She hurtles toward it, often turning back to see if or how far the police car's advanced.

Her smile is the petal of a marigold when it wilts when not exposed to sunshine and it's hope for her that's been pricked.

The man that had been trying to break into her house glares daggers into her soul, piercing through the layers and stabbing the dainty heart right in the centre.

"You..." her voice trails off as another man exposes himself. In a finely tailored brown suit and black hair gelled back into a manbun, is seated *Uncle Dallas*.

14

Realization slaps too late. She never had a relative named Dallas. She finds herself swimming in the cold blue waters of his eyes. It's enthralling, yet unnerving.

Something's not right. And before Risa can process anything, a deafening boom reiterates through the walls of the car. A body slumps on the ground, the gun slips from the jean pocket.

It was a *sickly game*, hadn't Uncle D said?

THE END

What Is Your Emergency

Donnie Ray

"911, what is your emergency?"

"Yes, I'm calling to report a murder," she said in a cold, distant voice.

"I'm sorry, ma'am. Did you say you're calling to report a murder?" asked the dispatcher.

"Yes," answered Victoria. She stared vacantly.

"I'm going to need some more details so I can send help. Let's start with your location. Can you tell me where you are?"

"No," said Victoria.

"You don't know where you are, ma'am?" asked the dispatcher.

"No," answered Victoria.

"Can you tell me what is around you? Is there anyone else you can ask?"

"No, I'm alone and it's dark," said Victoria.

"What's your name, ma'am?" asked the dispatcher.

"Victoria Dawson."

"Victoria," repeated the dispatcher. "Okay, Victoria. Can you tell me what happened?"

"I don't know," answered Victoria.

"You said you were calling to report a murder. How do you know there has been a murder?"

"Because I killed him."

"Okay," answered the dispatcher. "Victoria, I need you to stay on the phone with me." *Clack, clack, clack.* The dispatcher rapidly worked to track the location of the call. Only a general region in a heavily wooded area. The nearest county route was fifteen miles from where the dot was on the map. The dispatcher started her notes to the police. "I need you to tell me more about what happened. You said there was a murder and you killed someone one. Do you know the victim?"

"Yes, he's my husband."

"What is your husband's name?"

"John Dawson."

"Okay, and do you remember what happened to John?" asked the dispatcher.

"No."

"Are you near John right now?"

"No. I'm alone," Victoria repeated.

17

"Do you know where John is now?"

"No, I don't know where he is."

"Victoria, I'm sorry to ask so many questions but I need more information to know how best to help you. Now you said you're alone in a dark area and there has been a murder. You said you killed John, who is your husband. Can you tell me anything else about where you are or what happened?"

"We argued this morning before he left for work and I killed him," Victoria answered.

The dispatcher added this information in her instructions to the police unit on its way to the general area the call was coming from.

"What did you and John argue about?" asked the dispatcher. Maybe if he could keep her talking, he would get something more useful.

"He said I was spending too much money. But it was just a misunderstanding. He thought I was wearing a new dress, but it wasn't a new dress." Her voice trailed off.

"Okay, I have an officer on their way to your location. I'm going to stay on the phone with you until they arrive. Can you tell me anything else about what happened to your husband?"

"He was angry," she answered.

18

The dispatcher entered more information to the unit on the way to the location.

Somewhere in the night, two sheriff deputies were driving down a deserted county road. A thin mist hung in the air, in the beams of the headlights. The road seemed to absorb the light.

"This sounds strange to me," said the deputy from the passenger seat.

"What does?" answered her partner.

"Dispatch says it's a woman, alone, who reports she killed her husband after a domestic incident. But the woman can't tell them what happened or where her husband is now."

"Is dispatch sure about the location? I don't know who would be out here. There's nothing around here."

"Maybe she dumped the body and then decided to call herself in," suggested the deputy.

The dispatcher was getting nowhere with Victoria. She was clearly in shock. She spoke in a flat tone. Her voice was completely devoid of any emotion.

"Victoria, do you see any cars where you are?" he asked her, hoping the squad car was close.

"No, I don't see anyone," she answered.

The dispatcher tapped out instructions to the dispatched car. "I'm going to ask the officers en route to you to use their lights and sirens to help you see or hear them, okay Victoria?"

Out on the road, the deputy spotted the incoming instructions.

"Dispatch wants us to turn on the lights and sirens," said the deputy. Her partner pressed a couple of buttons on the dash. Flickers of red and blue reflected across the bare trees lining the roadway. The sirens echoed into the dark night.

"I think I hear something," Victoria told the dispatcher. "It sounds like sirens."

"Good," answered the dispatcher. "Do you see lights?"

"Yes, I think I see them."

"Are you near the road?" asked the dispatcher.

"No," responded Victoria.

"Can you get to the side of the road? The officers will have an easier time finding you."

"Okay."

The dispatcher heard crunching leaves and snapping twigs. The wailing sirens were faint in the background. He sent another message to the car to slow down. They were getting close.

20

"We're getting close. Sounds like she's somewhere in these woods. The dispatcher can hear the sirens on the call," said the deputy. Her partner let off the gas and the car slowed. The deputy scanned the sides of the road. "We may need to stop. I can't see a thing." Her partner eased the car to the shoulder of the road and came to a stop.

"Tell dispatch to tell the woman to head for the car." They got out of the car, pulling torch lights from their belts, shining them through the trees on either side of the road.

"Are you still with me, Victoria?" asked the dispatcher.

"Yes, I'm still here," she answered, slightly breathless.

"Good. Can you still hear the sirens?"

"Yes, they're louder now."

"Okay, good. The deputies are out near the road looking for you. Do you see the red and blue lights from the car or flashlights anywhere around you?" asked the dispatcher.

"Yes, I see red and blue flashes."

"Okay, good. You keep walking and head for the red and blue lights. I'm going to stay with you." *SPLASH*. "Victoria, are you okay?"

"Yes, I'm okay," she answered. "I stepped in a stream or a puddle or something."

"But you're okay?" asked the dispatcher again.

"Yes," she responded over the splashing of her steps in the water.

Up on the roadway, the two deputies worked slowly down both sides of the roadway, shining their flashlight beams into the trees.

"Do you see anything?" asked the deputy.

"Nothing on this side," said her partner.

"She can't be far," answered the deputy. "Wait, I think I see something." Her partner moved to the other side of the road, shining his beam to meet hers.

"How did she get way out here," responded her partner.

"Victoria?" called the deputy. The woman stumbled in the glare of the flashlight beams.

"I can't see," the woman called back.

The deputy lowered her beam to the ground in front of the woman as she made her way over a fallen branch. Her partner kept his beam up near the woman's face. He seemed frozen.

"Lower your beam," commanded the deputy. Her partner jerked his arm down. His wide eyes never left the woman's face.

When she finally broke through the tree line to the shoulder of the road, she stopped a moment. The deputy's free hand went to her holster. An instinct. The woman was wearing a long, ice blue, satin nightgown with a matching floral print robe. Her long brown hair was tangled around her head. Her hands hung at her side, still holding her cell phone in her right hand. The deputy glanced to her left, noticing her partner seemed frozen.

"Victoria, can you put your hands up in the air for me?" asked the deputy.

"She didn't kill her husband," said her partner suddenly.

"What? How do you know?" asked the deputy.

"She's my wife."

THE END

Captive

Lara Rosw

Subject 10000001284//:

Gender: Female

Age: 16

Full Name: Kiara Juna Bond

Preferred Name: Kiara

Family: Father, Chase Bond. Mother, Vivian Bond.

[ALERT indicated person(s) identified as missing]

Location: SYSTEM FAILURE

Jason aggressively clicked the keyboard mouse, as if reloading the page would unveil more information. The three dots would bob for thirty seconds before the system decided the impossible: It didn't have any information on Kiara Bond.

Her father's rebellion was predicted by the system - his headpiece detected anger when Chase was shown advertisements for anything technology related. By the time he had thrown his daughter's cell phone out the window of their 50th story apartment, the odds of running away peaked at 95%.

A warning was promptly sent out to the nearest Force base, and within an hour law enforcement was forcefully knocking on the door. The recommendation to detain Mr. Bond was the only warrant they needed - the system could be counted on. It caught crimes before they occurred, easily putting detectives out of business.

Kiara watched, her face stony, as her father fell limp without the Force stepping foot in the apartment. The system predicted the time they would arrive, predicted her father would be making dinner, chopping onions with a large government-issue knife. In avoidance of conflict, it simply sent the right electrical signals to send him into REM sleep. Her mother opened the door, her hand violently shaking. Kiara knew she would not fight, or the system would have disabled her as well.

Taking a single step away from the men, she stooped down to grab the discarded knife. It fit nicely in her fist, her fingers gripping the graphene hilt. The system immediately detected the unusual action, already monitoring the cameras. It tuned into her headpiece, collecting the data for later analysis. Weighing the chances she would do something violent, if it was more than 50 percent at any moment she would be on the floor as well.

-

But Jason, one of the many officials who used the system to locate and determine the motivation of perpetrators, was hitting a wall. Somehow Kiara was acting in such an erratic way as to fool the system. It would not betray the information of what she was feeling, or why she might have picked up the knife, without being certain on the statistics. However, while the system could not determine her next moves or motivations, the Force still had Kiara's tracker. If the force had not detained her yet, she would be found in a day.

Not wanting to leave his office empty-handed, but not having much of a choice, Jason packed up. The system was working constantly in the background, and if by the end of the day it didn't figure Kiara out, Jason would pay her a visit at the detention center.

-

Kiara was surprised the system had not disabled her as soon as she picked up the knife on the kitchen floor. But it wasn't her acting, otherwise, she would never have stooped down to grab the hilt. She would not have exited the apartment, taking the elevator all the way down to the old underground parking lot. Kiara would not have walked, barefooted, across the cement towards a lone gas vehicle. She would not have touched the dirt-stained handle to open the door and climb in, pulling the blindfold from beside her over her eyes. The system could not predict her movements because they were not **hers**.

She still had not dropped the knife, and a stab of pain cut through the side of her arm, the knife making a shallow cut. Dropping the knife, Kiara internally cringed at the loud clanging of metal on cement. Tried to focus on taking a step backward, moving in a way her anonymous captor did not facilitate. Instead, she pinched the cut until a small metal bulb came out. **A tracker**, she realized, **I just cut out my tracker**.

And by the time whatever trance she was in broke, she was blind, bound, and heading in an unknown direction. The system she and everybody else entrusted their lives to had not alerted the Force in time to save her. Because it didn't understand what she was doing, unable to factor in an outside force.

She was utterly alone.

-

"The tracker was cut out." Jason tried to explain to his boss, Martha, who was waiting outside his office. She believed he was slacking and had not done as much research as he should have. "We found it with traces of her blood in the abandoned underground lot under her apartment building."

Martha forced herself not to yell at Jason, he was only relaying the information. He was not responsible for the dead-end, only the bearer of bad news. "And the cameras?"

"We have her going down the elevator, looking panicked, but the cameras in the lot don't show her there."

"You're sure she took the elevator down to the lot? Didn't get out on the main floor, even through a back way?" Martha tried to keep the strain out of her voice.

Jason was irritated with her questioning, she spoke as if he had not considered the possibility himself. "I checked all of the footage." He was much more skilled at keeping emotions out of his voice. A perfect Force Head, relaying the information without opinion seeping through.

"What did the cameras on the parking lot exit show?" Martha was careful to phrase her words as to not be condescending.

"Nothing, the cameras were disabled hours before her father was even flagged." He was frustrated too, unable to solve the mystery. The system was short-circuiting with the effort of figuring out Kiara's motivation, and of no help. Nobody he had talked to had ever seen such a thing happen.

Jason was about to take a break for dinner when Vivian Bond broke through the doors of the unit, her curly hair filled with frizz and roughly pulled into a ponytail. "Put me under a truth detector, *now*."

-

The vehicle slowed to a stop, and Kiara barely managed to keep from slamming into the seat in front of her. After a few moments, the door beside her opened and four rough hands pulled her out of the vehicle. Despite the predicament, Kiara found relief in her physical ability to struggle against them. In the way, she could dig her heels into the pavement, before they dragged her and the skin rubbed against the rough surface.

Instead, she squirmed as much as she could, kicking the knees of her attackers. The effort did nothing except slow the speed at which they transported her, but when it became clear she would not cooperate, she was slung over one's shoulder. With each step he took, the impact drove his shoulder into her stomach.

Desperate and unwilling to go forward, Kiara flung her weight away from him. He allowed her to fall, but she had not thought far enough to predict the impact. The pain echoed through her, but only one thought was chorusing in her head. *Run, run, run.*

"You are a pain to hold onto." She heard one of them mutter as she stumbled, blindly running away from the pair. Managing to fling off her blindfold, blinding sunlight reflected off of the abandoned blue Walmart sign. Making the mistake of turning back, she saw the two men staring at her. One of them held a tranquilizer, and without seeing it fly through the air, a dart pierced her shoulder.

She fell limp once more, this time with the gift of unconsciousness.

-

Jason, with no more than a pause to evaluate Ms.Bond's mental state, rushed over to take her into the interrogation room. He had to brush the dust off the tables, as it had been abandoned for so long. Her arm was still shaking as he hooked up the most recent truth detector apart from the system. Its many wires suctioned to her forehead, collecting information through harmless radiation. When it was ready, he had his phone ready to immediately collect information.

"My husband was a member of a rebellion group, I think he called them the Secretum Society." She was rushing her words, and they were flowing over one another to create broken sentences. "He was always worried about being detained, saying something about Kiara. **Gods**, I can't remember what he said!"

"It's okay ma'am, calm down," Jason said, setting his hand on hers. Her eyes were still wild, but she was making the effort to breathe slowly.

"No! No, no this is bad, I wasn't supposed to tell you but Kiara's gone anyway and-" Her voice took on a desperate, pleading tone. "You have to find her, or they will kill her when they think my husband confessed this. Find her, you have to find her!" Ms. Bond burst into tears and was inconsolable. Jason stayed with her for half a minute longer, before opting to continue the investigation.

"What did she say?" Martha asked, waiting just outside of the interrogation room door. Of course, she could have checked the cameras, but it was usually the system's job.

But he just shook his head. "You should probably console her, she was too emotional to say much. I think she was just desperate."

Martha raised an eyebrow but did as he suggested. His heart was racing, but he just grabbed a Force hovercar and set the address of the abandoned Walmart on 22nd street.

-

Kiara awoke with a headache, and aftereffect of the tranquilizer the Force chose not to remove. It was a punishment, they explained to the press. For those who fought against being detained intended to break the law, and a headache is nothing in the grand scheme of things. But Kiara cursed the decision as a sharp spike of pain exploded through her skull. She thought it would be brought on by light, but a blindfold once again obscured her vision.

"Hello?" She called, her voice not echoing. Hearing another's faint breathing she continued blabbering. "I'm not sure why you are detaining me but I think you might have the wrong person because I don't know wha-"

"It's impossible for you to be the wrong person." A man's voice came from directly in front of her, the same one who shot her by the Walmart.

She considered his words for a moment. "Because you planned this. Because **you** were the one who controlled my movements! You-"

He cut her off again. "**You** need to stop talking before you say something that will get you killed."

Slumping in her seat, Kiara tested the strength of the metal handcuffs keeping both of her wrists behind her. She was sitting in a cool chair, likely an old metal one, not designed for comfort.

"What do you want from me?" She tried. There was no response. "How did you make me do things against my will?"

A cold barrel of an old-style gun pressed into her forehead, and immediately Kiara gasped and pursed her lips. There would be no more conversation.

The only thing capturing her attention was a gun fired in the distance.

-

Jason found four men leaned up against the old Wild Wing restaurant, dressed in clothes used before the Recycling. A faded pair of jeans which should have been given to the clothing department to be revamped into a more washable, durable fabric. Wearing such things would only mean they didn't care if people detected them breaking the rules. Because they had likely already done worse than keep clothing.

For a moment Jason debated turning back, but one of the men pointed at his figure, and two of them began making their way toward him. Whether he wanted to leave or not, it was too late.

Unfortunately, though they broke the rules, they had access to the latest technology. A tranquilizer whizzed past his forehead, they were shooting to disable. They wanted answers, Jason already had them. It took one shot of his ElecTro, and the air current around them was alight with energy. At once all of them, including the men at the door, keeled over in shock. Waiting until they went unconscious, Jason walked past their bodies and into the restaurant. Pressing the brick five down and two left from the top right corner of the wall, he sucked in a breath as a passageway opened.

"Freeze, and drop your weapon!" A deep voice came from beside him, and against his will, Jason froze for a second. Then he remembered he didn't take orders from members of the Secretum Society.

When he reached for his weapons, he found the attacker had already torn them from his belt. Jason was better trained, though, and launched himself on top of him before he had a chance to load the weapon. Grabbing the first thing he could find - an old pistol - Jason shot the man. The sound made his ears ring, but the man fell over. Jason was unharmed but barely escaped.

Descending into the cold, humid basement, he heard two sets of breaths to the left. As he pushed open the barn door with his foot, he was met with two familiar faces. Strapped into a metal chair, her mouth tight and lacking her usual smile, was Kiara Bond. Holding an identical old pistol to her forehead was Tyler, the same smirk Jason had burned into his memory.

"I see you were expecting me," Jason said gravely, loading the pistol from upstairs behind his back.

Kiara shrugged, and at the motion Tyler turned toward her, pushing the barrel harder into her forehead. She flinched at the movement. There she was, a hostage, and still, she tip-toed her way to danger, pushing herself further in a vain attempt at bravery. But her hands were bound, her legs tied together, and there was nothing she could do but hold her tongue.

"Chase was taken in for potential disobedience and rebellion, it was not voluntary. He didn't report you, you can let the girl go." Kiara sighed, she knew Jason well from when her father brought him over. He had yet to learn her name?

Tyler sneered. "So what brought you here, to try to valiantly save Kiara?"

Jason stirred at her name, making brief eye contact with her as if to apologize for forgetting it. She could not see through the black fabric. "I had prior knowledge of your plans."

The pistol was flipped around to face Jason, and Kiara's shoulders sagged in relief, but all logic was screaming it was not yet time to let her guard down. "A shame you had to die."

"No!" Kiara screamed, but it was not heard over the cracks of a gun firing, she could not hear over the ringing of her unprotected ears. Her eyes still blindfolded, she had no idea who was at the receiving end of the shots.

"Jason!" She called, mentally praying he was alive.

Never taking his hand off his shoulder, he dragged himself over to her chair and used his ancient swiss army knife to cut through the rope wrapped around Kiara's legs. At the motion, she relaxed and stopped fighting. Once they were free, he pulled himself onto his knees and removed her blindfold. Her eyes adjusted quickly to the dim basement, finding their way to Tyler's still body before jerking them away.

Jason slowly made his way to Tyler's body, fishing through his pockets until he found the key to Kiara's handcuffs.

It felt like an eternity before Kiara's wrists were no longer bound, but when she was free, she immediately shrugged off her sweater and crouched down to help Jason. He grunted in response to her putting pressure on his wound but did not say a word to dissuade her. Though she knew her position was one of danger, she would have no hope of getting out alive without him.

When Jason's shoulder was wrapped up roughly with her sweater, the pair slowly made their way up the stairs to ground level. What was not lost on Kiara was the way he still gripped the pistol, his mouth pursed in a straight line. While it was undoubtedly rude to talk, Kiara was not on the receiving end of a gunshot, so she felt freer to speak.

"You know why I was captured." She started, pausing with him as he stopped.

Jason turned to her, his brow furrowed. "You really should have stayed quiet, I almost forgot you were there."

"I get that a lot." Kiara shrugged but took a nervous step back after Jason began digging for something in his pockets. "What are you doing?"

"Trust me, this is better for everybody." It was an unfamiliar device, shaped like an ancient radio, but the antennae were cones made of flimsy plastic.

Kiara tried running, but he tackled her before she made it one step. "If you don't want them to kill you, you'll cooperate."

"Get off me!" Kiara struggled under Jason's weight, as the flimsy plastic suctioned to her forehead.

After a few seconds, she couldn't remember why she was fighting. Or where she was, she grasped for the memories but they slipped through her fingers, disappearing into the abyss. When she began asking a torrent of questions, the strange man finally rolled off of her. She didn't understand what occurred, but she followed the strange man into a Force hovercar, and he drove her all the way home.

THE END

37

Unpredictable Behaviors

Boba Bendy

You hate this. You hate living like this where your every mood can be understood by everyone. You hate how your life is predicated based on your behaviors. You hate how every time you try expressing something new, the only reaction you get is something you'd expect. Something you would predict. You just want to be... unpredictable.

It all started a few years ago when scientists developed a tool where everyone's behaviors could be predictable by someone else. Say your friend is talking about something, and they're trying to hide how they're really feeling about that topic. The person could tell how they're really feeling. Now everyone can go walking through the streets and talk to a complete stranger, yet know exactly how they feel. Know exactly what they truly feel...

You hate it.

People walk up to you, asking why you're so sad. Why your mind is so clouded that all you can think about is how much you hate that machine. Why your mind is so dark that you can't think about happiness anymore. Strangers want you to vent your feelings to them, change your behavior to make the world a better place. All you want is to have your emotions, your behaviors are secret again. You don't want a random person to walk up to you and ask, "Why so blue?" or, "Why so angry?"

The thing is, you can't be happy. Your whole life is an unfortunate event. The rare event that you have a good day is overruled by the unfortunate consequences that you've been through. Losing Cora, your house, everything you've ever owned. Getting treated like trash as you walk through the long, endless hallways of the school buildings. The hands that reach out to you, only to get pulled away when they realize who you really were. Saying things like, "Oh, I thought you were someone else" and, "Not like I'd reach for you anyway." Yet they always wonder why you're so temperamental, so predictable, so... different than all the other people. Everyone is supposed to follow the rules and only use the tool when they were allowed, yet you can always seem to tell when the basic girls use it on you secretly during tests and as you pass by them in the hallway with the hoodie over your head and your head hung low. Being told to stay behind after class, yet being the first one to leave. Refuse to stay, attempt to leave, they follow your behavior. All you wanna do is be unpredictable.

It was a long day at school. Tests, tools prodding at your sides, basics giggling and whispering, thinking they're being quiet but they're not. Long endless hallways where you lose your stacks of homework and sometimes lose your phone that you've kept in your pocket to avoid the embarrassing texts from your adoptive parents. The skin biting breeze as you're forced to sit by the open window on an overly crowded bus that has no volume control. Mumbling the words to your favorite song as everyone is trying out their new and improved tool on each other. Continue your prayers on the way home as the breeze snaps at your cold, red cheeks. Reaching under the mat that you never wipe your feet on, feeling for the cold, metal key, hoping to make it inside before your fears catch up to you on the front step of the apartment. Wrapping your fingers around the metal key, reaching out to put it in the keyhole of the lock. Whatever you do, don't turn around. Don't look the other way as you walk into the house. You close the door behind you, hoping that it wouldn't slam and awaken the family dog, whose behavior was one you didn't want to mess with. You set your black bag down by the shoe box, slipping off your navy blue and white checkered sneakers, making your way to the kitchen. Whatever you do, don't make noise as you open the door on the refrigerator and reach for the small box of apple juice. Sitting at the kitchen table only to be greeted by a note placed at your chair.

"Went to the store. Don't wake the dog. Dad will be back soon. Don't eat all the M&M's in the bowl" Love, Ashley.

Of course. She's always predictable. She didn't go to the store. She went on a walk just to get away from her stressful life. God, if you had only just packed your bag and went back to the CPS building. If only you could eat all the M&M's in the bowl. If only you could just get rid of all the tools in the world. No more poking into your mind and affecting your behavior from calm to pissed in less than 30 seconds. Every muscle in your tenses as you hear the front door of the apartment begin to creak open. Her humming was out of tune, yet she always made it sound good as she came in, earbuds in her pierced ears and her lips mouthing every word of her song. All you could think was, "Has she ever used the tool on me before?" When she looked at you, the circular tool in her hand, all you could see was her face pale and her hand began to shake in a form of fear. She showed the screen of her tool, that's when you understood why she was so afraid.

Now, normally, when one uses the tool, it instantly exports a word that would describe the person's behavior. Happy, angry, sad, all the predictable behaviors and words that typically contrast each other.

Blank. No words. Nothing but a glitch in the system to display... nothing. It finally happened, everything you've wished for. You watch as she shakily points at the door, yet you know what she meant. It hadn't been the first time she's done this. You nodded and walked to get your shoes from the shoe box, only for your ears to be greeted by a deep, low growl of the Rottweiler sitting on the couch, flaring its teeth at you. All you can do is just keep your eyes focused on the laces of your shoes, yet your fingers quicken their pace. Grabbing your school bag, you open the apartment door and walk out, listening to the click-clack of the nails of the dog across the floor, it's menacing growl approaching the other side of the door.

In due time, Ashley would call the police, telling them the situation. You'd be found, sent to laboratories to never see the light of the sun again as they experiment on how you're couldn't be predicted by the tool. The tool that never failed before. The tool with 5 stars internationally. As you walk down the sidewalk through the apartment neighborhood, feet going left, right, left, right, left, stop. Listen. Muscles all freezing in place as you hear the distant sound of the police. That's all you can do. You can't run, you can't hide, you can only freeze in place and hope that they don't suspect you as you act like you're texting on your phone. Everything inside is dark and twisted, yet all you can hope is that you're not the only one out there. Not the only one who wishes things were different. Sirens grow closer, prompting yourself to move, walk, speedwalk, run, sprint. Sprint toward the supermarket down the street where an ungodly amount of people would be, making it harder for them to find you. Run faster, they're going to find you. Listening to the gasps as people look at you, then their tool, only to see that their tool has malfunctioned and only showed a glitched-out screen.

How many people have seen you now? 20? 50? Run faster. All you can do is go out the front door of the supermarket and hope that they aren't waiting for you there. Left, right, left, right, left, right, quickened pace. Stop to wait for the automatic opening door to open, only to proceed sprinting out and into the sunlight and breeze. Down the sidewalk, sliding down the cold concrete into an empty canal, then sprinting under the bridge. Was this all worth it? To live your life running? To live constantly out of breath, yet to live with a new thrill in your body? What would Cora have thought? She would've said run... Besides, they took her for being unpredictable, why wouldn't they take you as well?

THE END

What would you like, sir?

Radhika Diksha

"Sir, we need you?"

"Ed, please don't panic, tell me what happened?"

"A man died at 4th Rose street in Pie- a- trust bakery."

"Pray, tell his name?"

"Robert Jr."

"Business tycoon Robert Jr.?" A sudden alarm switches on in my mind.

"You are right sir."

I hang up the phone, a new case is like coffee shots for me. Sudden shots of energy with a sudden smell of success. Being a private detective was tough in 1959, the remnants of World War were still haunting people's minds. So basically, everyone was behind food and money. Hence the rise of murders and death of rich men were the constant headline of newspapers and weekly magazines. The police were sometimes behind the culprit or were sometimes the culprit themselves. My first successful case was about Dorthy Maddaok, a murder mystery that had shaken the neighborhood. At that time, I was 19, who had only read Sherlock

Homes as his curriculum and used to write some articles for a newspaper column. Back then, I took the case for justice, not for fame or success. With my wit and observation, I nabbed the murderer to everyone's surprise and dismay. The success of the case made fame kiss my toes, but the police grew cold feelings towards me. First, the bitterness was one-sided, later with the continued collision of our thinking and ideas, it became a competition for us to prove each other wrong.

Coming to the case, Robert Jr. was famous as well as an established businessman. He was constantly in the newspaper due to the rounds of an affair between him, and a beautiful singer. The case was a gold mine for the press because now it had glamor and stardom.

I reach the spot, it was a small sit-in bakery with musty brown walls and white windows. It was unusual for a rich man to dine here, people were thronging outside the bakery to view the sudden death. Police were having a tough time trying to control the mob. I honk my Ford car on purpose, to gain the attention of the press. In seconds, a group of photographers and cameramen with their journalists were rushing towards my car. I took some time to come out of my car, but when I came out I was surrounded by the sudden flashes which blind my irises. There is a constant tugging and screaming of journalists at my face. I raise my hand to silence everyone, to bring their attention towards me.

"I will ensure that the culprit is caught, and the innocents are given justice. With the help of the police, we will solve the crime as soon as possible. Till then please maintain your integrity and work ethics."

I make a straight beeline towards the bakery. Where I'm coldly welcomed by Inspector Houston.

"Don't come here fella without any prior information. Take your media attention somewhere else," he smirks.

"It would be better if you pay enough attention to your duty, rather than observing my style and sensibility."

He stares at me and spits on the ground.

"So what are the details of the case, Mr. Houston?"

"According to the witness Robert entered the bakery with singer Sasha, they ordered a lime tart with lemonade. Then in the middle of the conversation, an argument burst open. A few seconds later he asks for water, which was given by Sasha from her bottle. In moments he clenched his head and passed out."

"So, where is the singer now?"

"She is in the basement of the bakery, hiding from the press."

"Bring in all the witnesses, and let's interview each one there itself."

We agreed to investigate the scene first. Nothing was weird nor there was anything suspicious. Then we interrogated each eyewitness.

First was the singer Sasha, a beautiful woman in her early 20's, with blonde hair and blue eyes. Her cheeks were stained by mascara, and her lips quivered from the constant crying. It was odd that a young girl like her was interested in a man who was in his late 40's, but it is not odd in a patriarchal society. I gave her my handkerchief, a man gotta respect a lady's emotion.

"So, Miss Sasha, what happened during your brunch at the bakery?"

"Robert called me here to discuss some private matters. He was stressed for the past few weeks."

"Can you guess, what he was about to discuss?" I ask.

She moves her head from side to side with few sobs.

"Miss Sasha when Robert asked for water. Instead, you could have called the waiter. Why did you provide it from your bottle?"

"Robert liked clean filter water. He always used to question the quality of water at restaurants, hence I used to carry my own source."

"Did you hand over the bottle to the police?"

She nodded.

The next person was the waitress, the only witness who was present at the bakery. A young woman in her mid-twenties, with hazel eyes and raven black hair. She was confident with her body language and was least affected by the sudden death.

"What's your name?"

"Rebecca Taylor."

"For how long you are working here?"

"Since the past few weeks."

"Can you describe what happened this morning?"

"Mr. Robert was coming to our bakery for the last few days, but this time he came with Miss Sasha. He ordered tart and she ordered lemonade. It's wrong to eavesdrop on anybody's conversation, so I was at my counter cleaning the stoves. But in the middle of their conversation, they started arguing. Mr. Robert was demanding Miss Sasha to leave her career. Then he asked for water, to which she gave her own bottle and in a matter of seconds he clenched his head and fell on the ground."

"Where was the owner of the shop?"

"Every morning the owner goes to buy the supplies for the rest of the day. He went out as usual."

The next person was the cleaner boy who was not the witness, but he was there in the basement of the bakery when the incident took place.

"What's your name?"

"Vayd Danish."

"So, Vayd Miss Rebecca told me that you went to the basement to take a puff of the cigarette."

Sometimes you had to twist other people's confession to extract the truth.

"No sir, Miss Rebecca had seen a few mice in our basement so, I went there to get rid of them."

"Ok, so for how long are you working here?"

"2 years."

Everything was done, we talked to the witness, we investigated the scene but couldn't find a clue. The police as well as I was waiting for the medical reports of the corpse, but it had a lot of time to it. Miss Sasha was on house arrest and other people were under observation. I took a few days to search for the missing links in this case but could not find one. This morning I decided to give a visit to the bakery. Through the glass windows, I could see Rebecca taking orders from the customer and Vayd helping his owner. I enter inside and Rebecca gasps her breath seeing me.

"Did I frighten you, Miss Rebecca?"

"No, I mean yes, the incident has made us face the worst fears that we never could have expected. What will you like sir?"She asks in a humble tone.

"Oh nothing, I just want to sit and relax for a few seconds, nothing else."

She goes away leaving me in silence, I try to connect the information that I had about this case, but couldn't figure out any missing links. A force knocks at my temples, the migraine bouts were reoccurring every morning. I press my fingers at my head to ease out the pain. I search my pockets for the container of pills, but I couldn't find them.

"Sir, are you okay?" I see Rebecca beside my table.

"Yeah, everything is fine, nothing to bother about."

She puts a tray in front of me, it has herb tea and strawberry custard.

"It's for your migraine sir, it will soothe your nerves."

I thank her and dig in my spoon because I have skipped my breakfast this morning. At the last spoon, a thought occurred to me. To clear it, I needed to meet the Dr. who was examining the body as well as the reports. I rush out of the bakery without paying the bill and race my car to the hospital.

"Dr. did Robert had a migraine? Because according to the witness he clenched his head before passing out. Did he get a migraine attack while having the arguments with the singer?"

"I don't know lad, maybe he had, maybe he hadn't. The technology isn't so developed to bring in the conclusions."

"What did you find in the reports?"

"The mystery is that we couldn't find anything with his body, the brain and his other organs were intact. But his blood reports are weird."

"What does the report say?"

"That during their argument there was the sudden spike of salts in his blood flow. He had large quantities of salts in his body during his death, which we call Hypernatremia. In Hypernatremia, a person typically feels thirsty. The most serious symptoms of hypernatremia result from brain dysfunction. Severe hypernatremia can lead to confusion, muscle twitching, seizures, coma, and death."

"So, how did this condition occur in his body, any clue?"

"We couldn't find that, but the bottle that Miss Sasha gave had typically weird ingredients and salts. I think you should further investigate it."

The police were informed about the reports and we both rushed to the villa of the singer who was currently under house arrest.

"Miss Sasha, we found salts and weird ingredients in your bottle and Mr. Robert died from Severe hypernatremia. The justice of sword points at you because before he had passed away, he demanded water from you."

"I drink salt-infused water to keep my voice intact and to keep throat infections away." She started to sob and pleaded in front of us that she was innocent.

She was taken in for police custody and the court will manage the rest of the hearing. We gave a press conference about the case and addressed questions of the media.

After a few days, I visited the bakery again to pay my pending bill and to meet the staff.

The staff members were happy to see me and greeted me with warm smiles, I paid my bill and talked to each staff personally.

Rebecca was happy and asked me about my migraine conditions.

"That day how did you know that I got a mild migraine attack?"

"My mother was suffering from migraine, so I recognized the symptoms really fast."

"So, you live with your mother?"

"No sir, my mother passed away a year ago. I live on my own."

"I'm sorry to hear about your mother, well take this."

I take 50 bucks from my wallet and hand it over to her.

"Take it as your tip and use it wisely."

She takes the money and her warm finger brush with mine, her cheeks tinge like strawberries, and she gives me a peck on the cheek. I smile at her and walk towards the door.

"Sir, please do come here again."

I turn around and say "I will come if I have time."

"I know you will." I nod to her and sit into my car, and drive to my home with a smile.

I was watching a soap opera on television while cooking my dinner. Then I hear a knock on the front door.

"Who is there?" I shout switching off the television.

"Sir, it's me, Daniel."

I take a sigh of relief and opened the door, Daniel was my counterpart as well as my personal spy. He used to track the backstory of the cases as well as the victim.

"So, Daniel what brings you here?"

"The back history of Robert Jr."

"Tell me the juicy details."

"He was a drug dealer in South Carolina and was once arrested while delivering a load of cocaine capsules."

"This businessman earns the white money with the help of the black money," I said.

"Listen, he used to execute his plans with a help of a female doctor, but after his arrest, she was absconding and still is on the wanted list. Here see her photo."

I take the file to view and my head spins, I reach the kitchen counter for support. I could not believe my eyes, it was Rebecca.

"What happened?" Daniel asked.

"She is the waitress who works at the bakery where Robert had died."

For a few seconds, we glared at each other and rushed to our cars.

I sped up my car not worrying about getting a fine. I rush into the bakery and shout.

"Where is Rebecca?"

Vayd rushes towards me with a note in his hand.

"Rebecca quit her job this morning and left a note for you."

I take the note and read.

Dear Thomas

Take a warm coffee with a heavy breakfast to curb your migraine attacks. Before sleeping drink a nice herbal tea, it will cure the migraine away.

And what else will you like, sir?

your friend

Rebecca

Something catches my eye across the street, and I rush towards the window to see clearly. It's Rebecca with red auburn hairs and a wicked smile.

She waves at me gives a flying kiss, and in the next second disappears.

THE END

 Flight Risk

Tom Humble

Since her official diagnosis with dementia, Gladys has wished to return to her birthplace while she can still remember her family members and landmarks. Her granddaughter has shown her around her old village on the computer, but it's not the same, of course. She wants to walk the cobbled lane to the family home one more time, feel the uneven stones underneath her feet. She can still manage a few steps on her own, so it is a possibility.

It is just past midnight, but Gladys is not aware of the time. The night sky is impossibly black against the bright deck lights. They are so bright Gladys can't see any stars, except for Venus. The moon is a curved sliver. Gladys' wheelchair is parked amongst the colourful deck chairs, a clunky thing of steel and rubber that her son has difficulty pushing around the cruise ship, so for the most part she is either in her room, in the dining room or out on the deck. She would like to visit the lounge and watch the people dance, even if she can no longer dance herself. She would also like to buy a mechanized chair, but she has overheard the added mobility could make her a flight risk as her dementia progresses.

The thought of being a "flight risk" when she can barely walk strikes Gladys as funny, but it is also frustrating, and is also terribly depressing. Sometimes she calls her son by her grandson's name, the boy who died as a baby in his crib: sometimes his name just slips out even though he died twenty years ago, and she can see the pain on her son's face but it means nothing in the moment because she has no idea why it would upset him. When he asks her later if she remembers what she said, Gladys says of course not, because she doesn't. This seems to pain him more, and he's been spending a lot of time in the ship's casino.

Gladys assumes that is where her son is now, plopping nickels in the slot machines, pretending everything is grand and probably flirting with the cocktail waitresses. Suits her fine; it is a lovely, clear night and she has her lapghan to keep her warm. The stern appears to be deserted; she could sit out here for hours, celebrity magazine open on her thighs, staring into the darkness and listening to the background rumbling of the engine.

Her solitude is broken by a young couple approaching from the left. She has seen them before: a good-looking couple, but quiet. The woman is very pale and very blonde, very thin and very downtrodden. Downtrodden is the right word: her eyes tend to stay down, on her food, on her hands; Gladys has even seen her boyfriend (husband?) pick and choose her food from the buffet line without a word from her. They have a strange energy, and people seem to give them space: they don't seem to be friendly with anyone else, and even the waitresses don't make small talk with them; they simply pick up their plates and leave.

The man is broad, looks like he works out in the ship's gym. Big head, buzz cut, muscular biceps, and has probably never smiled in his life. A waste of a handsome face.

Gladys looks down at her magazine but tries to keep them in her peripheral vision. The girl leads the way, arms crossed over her chest, head down. Her hair is back in a ponytail. She looks chilly in her little floral-print dress. The boy follows close behind in a pair of blue jeans and a tight grey shirt. They both glance at Gladys, who keeps her eyes on her magazine. They keep their distance from her.

Their voices are subdued; Gladys can't hear what they are saying. The boy seems angry about something: his tone is sharp; he pulls on the girl's arm and they stop along the handrail across from Gladys. They argue quietly for a bit, a long bit. He does most of the talking.

A pair of middle-aged women in short skirts walk through, giggling and chattering. Gladys wonders if they are single and whether they have perhaps flirted with her son in the casino. Her mind wanders back to her husband, long dead, who used to flirt with younger women, quite openly in fact. Many of them didn't seem to mind, he was such a handsome man and such a fluid dancer. Things are so different now than when she was a girl ... a girl with pretty dimples and bright eyes ...

Gladys is wakened by a muffled shriek. Her head jerks up; for a moment she's not sure where she is. She takes in the black sky, the bright lights overhead, the gleaming wooden deck. She wonders what time it is and how long she has been out here. Then she focuses on the couple, oh yes, the strange young couple having a quiet argument. It has become physical, she sees; the girl's feet aren't touching the ground. Her little white canvas shoes are being lifted up, up ...

Gladys makes a choking sound as she realizes what is happening. The man has deftly picked up his girl and she is now sitting on the handrail. One of her arms is around his thick neck, but in a swift movement she is over and out of sight.

The scene is frozen for a moment: he stands with hands braced on the handrail, head leaning over and down. Gladys stares at his back, her mouth an O, waves of terror washing over her, her mind going in four directions at once: *Did I really just see that? I need to call the police. I'm on a cruise ship.*

Please don't turn around and look at me.

She hears footsteps coming from one direction or another, she can't tell. Her head swivels around and there is her son, hair a bit disheveled, a look of contrition on his face. "Sorry Mom," he says. "I lost track of time." His hands are on the wheelchair handles; he unlocks the wheel brake with one foot and turns her around.

"Wait ..." The magazine falls from her lap onto the deck. She cranes her neck to see the man, who has already turned away from the rail and is now sauntering away in the opposite direction, one hand in a pocket as if nothing has happened. Nothing at all.

"I hope you don't catch cold," her son says. "It's kind of chilly out here." He steers her through the automatic door.

"Did you see that man?" Gladys asks. She tries to twist in her chair to look her son in the eye.

He glances down. "What man?"

"The man with the girl."

"What? I didn't see a girl." He wheels Gladys down the carpeted hall and to their cabin. As he slides the key card into the lock he asks, "What girl? Did someone sit with you for awhile? Keep you company?" He pushes the chair into the room and pulls the lapghan from her legs. "Are you thirsty? Would you like some juice?" He balls the blanket up and tosses it on the foot of her bed.

"No!" Gladys' face flushes with frustration. "I want-"

"Oh shit, I forgot your meds. Hang on." He disappears into the bathroom and returns with her weekly pill organizer and a glass of tepid water from the sink. "There." He smiles with satisfaction after she has swallowed her pills. "So who sat with you out there tonight?"

Gladys stares at her son, hand automatically rearranging the invisible blanket on her lap. She opens her mouth, but the words she'd planned to say are gone. Her head droops: suddenly she is so tired, she simply cannot keep her eyes open.

"Alright," her son whispers. He retrieves the lapghan and spreads it over her legs. Then he removes her shoes and gives her feet a quick massage. "Nap in the chair. We'll get you in bed later." He gives her a light kiss on the cheek and gets himself ready for bed. One more day on the high seas and they will be in Scotland.

THE END

Boogeyman

Ximena Chavez

My vision became hazier by the second and the only thing that I could make out of it was the scary lady with a gun in her hand that stopped short in front of me. I listened to the weary sirens in the distance and the cries for help sounding somewhere far from here. I felt like I was losing myself, like I was dying. I could only faintly remember what happened before I blacked out. I remember a girl. A young one. She was about 11 years old with blue-gray eyes and long black hair. I remember her saying only one thing to me. It was a name. A name that started with a B. B-B-B....It was impossible. I couldn't remember the name. "Julien Dolores you're under arrest for the kidnapping of Harper Lennox, first degree murder, and first degree assault. You have the right to remain silent. Anything you say can and will be used against you in a court of law. You have the right to talk to a lawyer and have him present with you while you are being questioned. If you cannot afford to hire a lawyer, one will be appointed to represent you before any questioning if you wish. You can decide at any time to exercise these rights and not answer any questions or make any statements. Do you understand each of these rights I have explained to you?" I gave the scary woman - who I now know is a police officer - a weak nod yes. "Please respond with a yes or a no or another form to get your consent." I turned to give the woman a dreary eyed look and I sputtered out the word yes. "Having these rights in mind, do you wish to talk to us now?" My mind rolled into loud bangs of thunder as I caught on to a couple of brief memories of what happened last night. I was being arrested. And I wasn't the one who did it. It was him. It was the Boogeyman.

The police officer that had arrested me was standing right in front of me when I opened my eyes. I took in the scent of the polished room. The smell was putrid. It smelled of wet cement and dead fish. There were a couple of brochures with all of the titles including 'possible parole' in them, and an end table holding a coffee maker and an old fashioned telephone. My senses kicked in when I eyed the telephone and my memories slowly seemed to be flooding back into my brain. "I see that you've finally woken up." The police officer stared at me with cold eyes. I stared right back. "So, you wanna tell me exactly what happened, or do you need a little bit of motivation?" The scary lady had on a name tag. Her name was Darcy. "Officer Darcy, please, you have to believe me. I didn't murder Harper Lennox. If it's still the same day, I was coming home late from work last night calling in on a few clients of mine. It was around ten o' clock when I left the office. I hopped into my car and started driving. As you could probably imagine, I was really tired and I was just trying to get home faster so that I could get home to my kid. So, instead of taking the usual route that I take to get home, I took a detour."

"And where exactly did this detour lead to?" Officer Darcy wasn't buying into it. "The detour wormed through a sketchy neighborhood. There weren't many people around, just a couple of dogs and drunk adults."

"I'm going to have to interrogate the people who live around there. See if there are any witnesses. If you're lying it'll only be worse." I was really working her up and I barely started speaking. I wonder what she'll say when I bring up the Boogeyman. I'm dead. No doubt. "Please, just listen. I kept getting the feeling that something wasn't right, like something bad was going to happen. And then it did. I heard someone screaming. They were blood curdling screams that made my skin crawl. I couldn't just leave them there, not while they were helpless. I rolled down my window just a bit to be able to follow the screams. I was led to an alleyway that was surrounded by a bunch of dumpsters and a pile of cigarette stubs. I honestly even started to reconsider my decisions when I got off of my car. I stayed put for a minute or two just to make sure that I wasn't hallucinating. The screams had stopped, but then the strangest thing happened. I don't know what it was but whatever it was, was what murdered Harper."

"So you're telling me that something, not someone, murdered an innocent 11 year old girl?"

"No, that's not what I'm saying. I swear that it wasn't me. This thing crawled out of somebody's apartment window and it was holding her. I followed my instincts and I ran after it. The thing that had Harper ran faster than any normal human would be able to, it may even have been flying. It stopped in front of a building that had a bunch of graffiti on it. The one where you found Harper dead. Harper was crying and she was so scared. She begged me for my help and of course I did my best to help her out, but she kept saying a name. A name that started with a B. She called it the Boogeyman. And I don't know what it was that I saw but by the time that I tried to figure it out, Harper's vocal chords were ripped out of her throat. They were splattered all over the ground. Her blood was everywhere and Harper stood up. She was still alive, but all the while she was still screaming in undeniable pain. She dipped a finger into her pool of blood and wrote something on the wall behind her with it." I seemed to be getting to Officer Darcy, although she still didn't seem entirely convinced. She had a look of fear but also a look of doubt. Then she said something. She almost whispered it. "What did she write?"

"It's on the camera roll of my cell phone." The officer pulled out my phone from a plastic bag and opened up my camera roll. Her face turned completely white when she read it. Do you want to know what the note said?

I won't yell at mommy ever again.

Officer Darcy left the room to speak to a lawyer for me. She said that she didn't know what to believe. She said that my story didn't make sense. I'm anticipating the moment when I have to attend my trials. There is a 99.9 percent chance that the jury will read the verdict and it will declare me guilty. The other 0.1 is the one chance I have that somebody will believe me and get me out of this nightmare. Officer Darcy explained to me her side of the story. She said that my DNA was all over Harper's body. They even found a dagger on the scene with my fingerprints on it and have security camera footage of me slitting Harper's throat open with the dagger. I was drowning in my thoughts until I heard a knock at the door. It was my daughter. My heart melted and my eyes stung with tears. She forced herself to come into the room and took the seat across from me. "Dad...what happened?" I couldn't even look Paulina in the eye; she probably considered me a scumbag just like everyone else. "I didn't kill that poor innocent girl. Paulina, please, you have to believe me. This place-these people are driving me insane. They're pulling hard evidence out of their back pockets and every single piece of it all gets pinned back on me. I just don't understand what's going on. I'm being framed. I know I am." Paulina didn't look upset or even worried. In fact, she seemed calm and put together. She softly inhaled and said, "I do believe you. I know that you would never do something like that and I promise it on my life that I'm going to get you out of here. But I can't do it if you're not willing to do whatever it takes." I gave Paulina an affirmative nod. I took a quick glance at the bored officer that was lazily standing in the back and I drew an x across my chest. Paulina smiled at me and said her goodbyes. She gave me one last look before she shut the door and then I was all alone again.

This prison was really depressing. Peeling walls, stained floors, dim lights, and then to top it all off, the vexed inmates. At least Officer Darcy was kind enough to escort me to my luxurious prison cell. Officer Darcy sorted out the details with me about my lawyer and scheduled a meeting time with her tomorrow morning at eight o' clock. She informed me on some of the prison rules and then left me in the cell. I was given my own cell with no roommate since the officers were kind enough to classify me as a category A prisoner. "Alright, delinquents! Lights out!" This whole thing was totally botched. I didn't deserve to be here. I dragged myself to the rectangular piece of metal that was supposed to be my bed and I draped my eyelids shut.

I woke up drenched in sweat. I searched for a clock between the bars of the cell. It was 2:57 in the morning. I couldn't slow my breathing down and my fingers were all trembling under the soupy weight of my body. I had a terrible nightmare; it was about him. The Boogeyman. I remember that he was seeping in under the cracks of Harper's door back in her apartment and she was sound asleep. I tried screaming her name, furiously shaking her, but she wouldn't wake up. The boogeyman ominously towered over her frail body and whispered something so quietly that I almost missed it. "You've been a very bad girl. I'm sure that mommy isn't very happy." Harper woke up when she heard the demonic voice. She whimpered and said that she was sorry. That she would never do it again. "You hurt mommy's feelings when you yelled at her and said those awful things…" Harper couldn't speak; she just sat there, paralyzed with fear. The Boogeyman swept her off her feet and told her that he would teach her a lesson in his hissed, horrendous voice. But it was like he could sense that I was there. He stared directly at me with those lifeless eyes and his sharp, jagged teeth. When he charged toward me, I woke up. I shook off my fears and I got back into bed. I shut my eyes as hard as I could and threw the blanket over my head. The trial was in two days, not even my wise, intelligent daughter could get me out of here. I was slowly being lulled to sleep by the mechanic whirs of an air vent nearby but then a noise interrupted me. It wasn't just any noise, it was a scream, and it was coming from the end of the hall. I reluctantly inched toward the bars and peeked through them. The color from my face drained and my whole body went numb when I saw it. It was him. He just murdered someone else.

It was the man that I passed by when I was being escorted to my cell yesterday. He was in his mid twenties, dreadlocks, and covered in tattoos. He was in pieces. There was a pool of blood around him and he was sitting outside of his cell. I gagged to myself, but then it got worse. There were words. And they were written in his blood. "I'M SORRY FOR CHOPPING MY GIRLFRIEND INTO PIECES." I was terrified. I backed into the darkest corner of the cell praying that he wouldn't get to me too. One after another, the screams got worse and worse. Where were the guards? I cried silent tears and listened closely for another scream or another cry. But there was nothing but the eerie silence and the whisper of air tickling my ears. I couldn't move. I waited for another five minutes until I decided that I had to do something, **anything**. I stood up and I reached for the lock on the cell. I reached for the bobby pin in my pocket that I found earlier hidden in here between a crack in the wall. I picked the lock until I heard a reassuring *click*. I searched frantically for a guard or someone to help me but everyone in this unit was dead. I sprinted in the direction of Officer Darcy's office. But I stopped short when I saw who was in there with her. Paulina was in there, but why was she here? And why was she here at three o' clock in the morning? I was just about to place my hand on the door handle when I heard shallow breathing. It was cold. It was so cold. I shivered and waited for whoever it was to show themselves. "Who's there?" No answer. Two minutes. Three. No answer. I proceeded to open the door. "Don't go in there." Someone cackled. "Do you want to know why Paulina is here?" The voice continued to hiss but never came out of the shadows. "Who are you? And how do you know my daughter's name?"

"I think that should be the least of your problems." The voice seemed to be mocking me. It sounded like I was bringing amusement to it. "She's here to help the officer put you behind bars....for good. Don't believe me?" I was too late to run when I realized that it was the Boogeyman. He sped towards me and grabbed a hold of me. I looked him into the eyes and I saw everything. *Paulina spoke to Officer Darcy before she came to see me. It was horrible. I didn't want to believe it. She told her that I was dangerous. A scumbag. That I didn't deserve to live.*

She was helping her put an end to me and she was planning to from the very beginning. I didn't even need to ask Paulina if it was true. I knew that it was. I wanted to kill her. I wanted to cut off her lying tongue and bash her skull into a pile of rocks. I wanted to squeeze her neck and watch her get on her knees and plead for her life. I was angry. So angry. I didn't even care about the Boogeyman anymore. For once, I wish I *was* the Boogeyman. "Go teach her a lesson...she deserves it." I engulfed him and I fed on his every evil intention. I kicked down the door to the office and grabbed both Officer Darcy and Paulina by their throats. "Kill them all." I hissed at the Boogeyman. His lips curled upwards. "With pleasure." I dragged the two wretched snakes by their hair and forced them up with me to the roof of the building. The cold air felt replenishing to my skin and I threw the two helpless peasants onto the ground. As I anticipated, they both begged for me to let them live. *You're not you* blah blah blah *you don't want to do this* blah blah blah *you're not a killer* blah blah blah. Oh, but I do want to, and I am a killer. "First, let's begin with you, Officer Darcy. Paulina shall' be my dessert." I drowned out the sounds of Officer Darcy's pleas. I gave her a parting smile and stabbed her right where her charcoal rock of a heart was placed. Her blood splattered all over my face. This was quite enlightening. I threw her over the roof and watched her splat on the ground like a blob

71

of jelly. Paulina was crying miserably. As she should. I walked over to her and kicked her in the face. "Daddy, please. Don't do this! I promise that it's not what you think! Whatever that thing told you was a lie! I promise!" I hated that I still had love for this rat. I choked her until she barely had life to hang on to. She cried and pleaded but I didn't care. I stabbed every part of her body and I laughed every time she screamed. I let her bleed out, and once I knew she was dead I gripped one of her fingers and dipped it in her blood. I wrote one sentence. "I WILL NEVER BETRAY DADDY EVER AGAIN." I spit in her face and I left her there. She was dead to me. Mentally and physically. The Boogeyman appeared and cackled at the sight of Paulina. ""She'll do nicely in my collection."

"Collection?" The Boogeyman let out another cackle and stared at me. "You're quite gullible, aren't you?" He walked towards me and just stared with at me with those eyes. My brain burst into a thousand pieces and my blood was everywhere. I wasn't sure what was happening but it seemed as though I couldn't control my body. I dipped a finger into my blood and wrote down a note. I collapsed to the floor when I finished and the Boogeyman disappeared with a horrid sneer. Do you want to know what the note said?

Don't ever trust the Boogeyman.

THE END

Veil

Skyler Woods

Fernando didn't kill his son, Adam. But everyone believed he did. He had to clear his name and prove his innocence. He also had to rescue his son. Fernando spent time inside of a maximum-security state prison.

But tonight was a special night. Fernando's wife helped him escape prison. Fernando had bruised and bloodied knuckles from knocking the daylights out of a prison guard. Fernando never punched a man before. He fractured a man's jawline and broke his nose.

A few days ago, Fernando killed the Devil. Since the Devil is a supernatural being, shooting him or stabbing him would silence him only for a little while. The Devil tricked Fernando after a chief military scientist unleashed the evil being on Fernando. He made him believe that he was going back in time to save his son. A top-secret government experiment that went wrong. Fernando also found out that a colleague set him up with the Devil's help.

Fernando's wife, Leona, had connections with a highly advanced and classified military organization. She worked as a counter-terrorist agent for the FBI for eight years and she soon worked her way up through the CIA's top-secret level divisions.

Leona tried to save her husband from getting arrested, but the classified military government she worked for apprehended her. They gave her two choices. Allow her husband to be arrested for something he didn't do or let him get killed by a sniper's bullet. They forced Leona into choosing to allow the government to frame her husband for the murder of their child. Leona knew who killed their child, but it was a government coverup. A time machine fueled by witchcraft could not be exposed to the public. The military organization arranged a time-traveling mission to look like a crazy father who murdered his only son.

"Will we get there in time?" Fernando asked his wife through his nervous breath. Inertia pushed Fernando back in his seat whenever his wife would punch the accelerator. It was midnight, and the 5.2-liter V10 engine in his wife's sports car roared wildly down a lonely highway.

"We're gonna make it. My men are at the facility, waiting for my signal." Leona projected confidence through her gentle voice. She briefly reached over to caress her husband's hand. But within a second she placed her hand back on the steering wheel, forcing her mid-engine Audi R8 to swerve between two semi-trucks.

The voice of the rap star, Lil Baby, boomed softly out of the sound system in Leona's sports car. Leona pushed her sports car to its maximum rpm.

"There are 200 men with automatic rifles guarding the perimeter," Fernando spoke smoothly while pulling out his gun, reloading new bullets into its magazine clip. "If we get past the armed guards, we'll need the code to get inside the facility. We must get through the impenetrable vault that's underground where the Veil is being kept. There are ten guards outside the vault." Fernando knew that anything was possible, but he feared the worst. He tried to reflect on his wife's confidence. It was hard since his wife was an army woman and he was a wrongly disqualified military scientist.

"We'll make it through," Leona's confident words exceeded her anxiety. "Remember, we used to work at the facility before they terminated us. We were a part of the team that created Project Romulus. You helped with the engineering of the Veil. We know how to make our way through that facility, because it's familiar territory for us," Leona spoke through a precise half-whisper while swerving between cars and punching the accelerator.

"Is God judging us for using the Veil to bring back our little boy?" Fernando knew his question was absurd, especially when he saw his wife shake her head at him.

"Sweetheart, why would God judge us for using your time machine to save our baby? God knows that our son was kidnapped and murdered. Why would he give us even more pain by judging us? God helped you with the Veil. The Romulus organization funded your project. The Veil was your machine, they just took some of the credit for it. We had a right to use the Veil to save our child." Leona inserted justification into every word. Leona was right. The Veil was her husband's machine. It used the psyche of a demon spirit to create time traveling missions. Since angels and demons are ancient beings that never really die, they go through time, keeping a track record of every moment in life. Leona helped her husband build a machine that could capture those spiritual track records.

"Every day I think about that serial killer. I think about what he did to our Adam," Fernando stated. He often thought about how he came close to stopping the masked killer from breaking into their house. He almost stopped the kidnapper from killing the babysitter and abducting their son. But then something happened. Something that Fernando couldn't explain. Fernando remembered when he first used the Veil to rescue his son. When the Veil activated, a dimensional vortex manifested and a demon was summoned using a witch's spell. The spell forced the demon to keep the vortex open.

"I keep thinking about the killer too." Leona whispered to her husband, trying to calm her nerves. Leona remembered that day vividly. She remembered witnessing a witch scientist summoning a demon into the Veil and her husband placed a hold on him using a harness with a crucifix attached to it. Her told the demon what period he want to go back to and the witch forced the evil spirit to open a wormhole within the Veil's quantum stabilizer bars, which kept the demon's power from destroying the Veil and it also prevented the wormhole from becoming a bomb. Leona thought about how someone set her husband up after he stepped into the wormhole inside the Veil. She wanted to go with him. She wanted to help rescue their son, but he told her to stay behind. After Leona watched her husband step into the Veil, two armed guards approached her and escorted out of the room against her will. "Somebody double-crossed us," Leona told her husband while reflecting on what happened. "Someone lifted the crucifix hold on the demon that created the wormhole you traveled through. I don't think the witch did it. That demon or possibly the Devil was set free inside the Veil by someone on the engineering team. The demon went into the vortex, possessing our son and attacking you. You tried to kill it, but you accidentally killed our baby." Leona stopped talking when her husband let out a grieving moan.

"Do you know who did it?" Fernando gritted his teeth. He gripped the handle on his gun which was resting on his knee. Fernando couldn't stop thinking about how close he came to saving their son.

"I think I know," Leona answered. She effortlessly pushed her German sports car up to 102 mph. "I think it was Chief Commander Gary Bautista. He was the head of Project Romulus. I think he got jealous when you won the Horizon Award for your design of the Veil," Leona explained her theory. Commander Bautista always envied you." Leona had another explanation behind why her husband was framed. She kept her other explanation to herself. Guilt prevented Leona from telling her husband the true reason he was framed for murder.

A brief silence occurred. Within the silence, Leona thought about her son. She thought about when her baby learned how to walk. Adam followed his mother around the living room after he left his father's arms. Leona would never forget how Adam giggled while waddling toward her with his miniature arms reaching out to her. When Leona scooped Adam into her arms, she never thought in her wildest dreams that she would hold her baby for the last time. Her husband didn't know that a serial killer would take the life of his son a week later.

"I keep seeing his face," Leona broke the silence, bringing up their son. The mother cried so many times over their child's death that she lost count.

"I see his face too. I see him every day." Fernando rumbled out his words through a whispering tone. He gazed at his wife while reaching over to touch her knee. When Fernando reached over to touch his wife's knee, his fingers bumped into the handle of the 38 caliber pistol strapped to her leg beneath her sparkling blue velvet dress.

"We're gonna save him this time." Leona's British accent and her gentle tone of voice emphasized her words. "God helped you build the Veil so we could save our baby. Nothing's gonna stop us. Not a demon, or the Devil, or an envious lead scientist is gonna stop us from saving our son!" Leona's silky voice increased in volume. "I want to see my little boy's eyes again. I want to hold him in my arms before this night ends. We have all the weapons we need to accomplish this mission." Leona boldly took her eyes off the road to look at her husband. She slowed her sports car down while taking her husband's hand. Leona and her husband weren't afraid of dying. Saving their little boy from a serial killer was worth inviting death to their doorstep.

◻①◻

Night shielded an invisible task force team. A team of men zeroed in on a group of armed guards near a perimeter gate. The armed guards never knew what hit them. An armed guard tried to defend his fellow man, but an unseen force flipped him on his back. The force snatched his machine gun right out of his hands. The armed guard saw nothing. He only heard a deep voice telling him to stay down. When the soldier disobeyed the voice, he paid the hard way. He attempted to rise while reaching for a handgun strapped to his waist, but he fell back down when the unseen force shattered his kneecap. When the armed guard fell back to the ground on his broken leg, he was about to scream out in pain but a serrated knife blade sliced his throat.

This happened to the other armed guards. They'd watch something unseen smoothly disassemble their machine guns while it was still in their hands. Before they could alert their superiors, they would die either by a knife entering their throat or by two hands dislocating their neck. Every armed soldier was getting flipped on his back and executed. Since the soldiers couldn't see what was attacking them, they felt like the night sky had come down to kill them.

Not a single armed guard pulled the trigger on his machine gun. They were being silenced by highly skilled invisible ninjas.

Chief Commander Gary Bautista saw the commotion happening near the perimeter gate on one of his CCTV cameras. He grabbed his gun while stepping out of a watchman chamber inside a vault where the Veil was concealed. A deep, thunderous voice emerged from inside of the Veil, stopping Commander Bautista in his tracks.

"Someone wants to take your power," the dark voice echoed out of the mountainous machine. It spoke through a half-whisper, but it still shook Commander Bautista's eardrums.

"Who wants to take my power?" Commander Bautista asked the voice. He walked up to the Veil after pressing a button on the machine's door and watching as a metallic shield on the door slid open to reveal a 7-foot tall humanoid monster, that had a bronze harness across his muscle-bound chest, with a crucifix attached to it. The monster had twisted thorns growing out of his forehead. He had long mangled white hair that drenched his broad shoulders. His skin had snake scales and it was pewter gray. His eyes were a hot molten red and his face resembled the appearance of a decaying corpse.

"You can't hold power forever. Infinite power will slip between your fingers like sand." The evil entity leaned forward while giving Commander Bautista a snarling smirk through the Veil's transparent explosion-proof door.

"But you're the Devil. You know how to hold on to power," Commander Bautista spoke back to The Beast almost in a hypnotic trance.

"I'm limited!" The monster roared at the chief military scientist. He tugged on the bronze harness that kept him held down to a bolted seat. "You used a witch to put a hold on me. The spell of a witch and this crucifix keeps me imprisoned inside this stupid machine. I'm not God. He would never subject himself to such torture!" The Beast dug his claws into a concrete wall behind him. "Even I've allowed my power to be vulnerable. A puny mortal man like you shouldn't be able to hold me." The colossal muscles in the monster's arms and chest would twitch every time he would speak and growl.

"I'm sorry, but you're the battery. You're the Veil's power source. Man has always dreamt of being the master of time. Now that dream is a reality." Commander Bautista was so intrinsically captured in his conversation with Satan that he wasn't aware of two invisible soldiers lurking behind him. It was a man and a woman. A husband and wife dressed in state-of-the-art military gear.

"Your dream will end in a few seconds," The Beast told Commander Bautista through a mocking whisper. He stroked his claws across his chin, knowing that Commander Bautista was about to die.

One slice across the throat was all it took. Commander Bautista's sturdy body dropped to the floor. Blood spurted out of his throat, painting his silver beard.

"That was quick." The Beast chuckled, tapping his claws on his knee. He shifted his glowing crimson eyes between the woman and the man. "Well, look at this. It's Adam and Eve." The Beast threw his head back, releasing a ground rumbling laugh.

"We need you to open up a timeline!" The woman who was Leona removed her bulletproof helmet while shouting her orders to The Beast.

"Everyone needs me to do something, now don't they?" The evil creature's words and his unrelentingly deep voice sauntered in the air.

"It's about our child," Fernando told the Devil while removing his armored military vest and revealing the tattoos on his bulky chest, that a black tank top partially concealed. "A man killed our son on August 4th. It was on a Friday at 7:15 pm. We need to go back to that date and we need you to send us ten minutes before the time of our son's death." Fernando watched as The Beast looked him up and down while chuckling.

83

"You forgot to say please." The Beast folded his massive arms while leaning back in the seat. He waited to hear the word emerge from Fernando's mouth, but he heard it from Leona's lips.

"Please help us." Leona looked the Devil in his eyes while removing her military vest. She knew The Beast would lust after her as soon as he saw her blue dress hugging her shapely body.

"For you, my child, I'll do anything." The Beast flirted with Leona. "I have to help. I'm trapped in this machine and God's will is always stronger than mine." The Beast stretched forth his hand, creating a swirling dimensional tunnel within the Veil's quantum stabilizers. The tunnel looked like a horizontal vortex made of lightning.

"I'll stay here and keep watch on him." Fernando diverted a glance at The Beast. "You rescue our child. You save our Adam and you'll clear your husband of murder. You'll change our future." Fernando gave his wife a timeless kiss, before releasing her hand and watching as she slowly made her way inside the Veil toward the swirling vortex.

Leona entered the Veil, with her gun clutched in her left hand. She gave her husband one last look, and she rolled her eyes at The Beast before entering the vortex. When Leona dived in, she felt every cell in her body pulsate. In an instant, Leona stood in the living room of her home. She terrified the babysitter who was standing in the kitchen holding Adam. The teenage girl couldn't believe that she saw Leona appear out of thin air.

"It's okay, Sweetie!" Leona told the babysitter. She didn't know that the serial killer was already in the house and was standing right behind her. Leona turned around at the right time and she unloaded every bullet in her gun into the man's body. After shooting the serial killer multiple times, Leona approached the man's body. She removed his mask to see that it was Commander Bautista. The chief scientist was still alive and he stared up at Leona with utter shock in his eyes.

"You're supposed to be out having dinner with your husband tonight! Tonight's your marriage anniversary." Commander Bautista choked out his words. His enormous body convulsed when Leona dropped her knee on his chest.

"Did you think you could kill our baby tonight?" Leona leaned down into the killer's face with her hands wrapped around his throat. "I didn't want to be unfaithful to my husband anymore. My husband can't know that I cheated on him with you. You broke into my house and killed my two-year-old baby because I rejected you. My husband kills you in the future. But I'm gonna kill you right here in the past. You die twice." Leona blew a kiss down at the man she cheated on her husband with before putting a bullet into his skull. While releasing a sigh of relief, Leona slowly rose to her feet after removing the murder weapon from the killer which had her husband's fingerprints planted on it. Leona turned around to face the babysitter. When she saw her son in the babysitter's arms, she wanted to hold him. But the vortex was still in the living room, and it sucked Leona back into the future. As Leona traveled back into the Veil, she had the comfort of knowing that she freed her husband, and that she would see her Adam once again.

THE END

Fall Of the Stars

Steve Harold

The heavens glittered with stars as the man silently drove over dirt and gravel, the thousand twinkling eyes mocking his desperation.

Muttering a curse under his breath, he slowed down at the rusty security gate at the entrance of the abandoned mines. To an ordinary person it would be a half-broken gate with just a couple of night guards sleeping their shift away. But then again, the average person wouldn't notice that the old equipment was strewn about almost too cleanly, or that the uniformed guards lacked an identity or a logo.

Or how a cold eye glinted from under the angled cap, a sleek gun pointed at any approaching vehicle. Private security.

Good, he smiled. He'd expected nothing less.

He rolled down a window and casually brought up his right hand to scratch his stubble, flashing them the tattoo on his arm. One of guards came over to inspect it, shining a flashlight right in his face. Satisfied, he nodded to the other one, and the gate opened.

The newcomer growled at them as he drove past. The guards didn't blink.

He took the car to the mouth of the mines and parked it aside a vintage piece, tossing the keys inside when he got out.

Won't be getting out in this ride, that's for sure.

He took one last look at the night sky. The stars still winked at him. *I'll show you, you damned twinklers,* he thought. *And then you and your glowing arses can collectively burn the fuck out.*

He walked in and took the narrow elevator down, fixing a crick in his neck to look at the small black camera from the corner of his eye. The caged door opened into a tunnel entrance sealed long-ago. Dim light and vulgar music blared from within.

The tunnel widened into a narrow hall within, a despicable den of sin. Sellers had set up their wooden stalls on either side, sporting wares of all kinds and catering to the needs of anyone bold or foolish enough to venture within.

A place fit for the lowest of low-life scum, the kind who'd kill their own mothers for the right price. Everything in the hall was as good as Eden's forbidden fruit on Earth, attracting a number of fools who'd end up unconscious in dirty alleys, pickpocketed at best, missing an organ or an appendage – if not sporting a slit throat, at worst.

The market and its dealers had been thriving in the sealed mine for almost a decade now, and he had no doubt that even the poorest of these merchants could have half the law enforcement in their pockets.

He grunted. *Hell, half the buying and betting crowd out here was law enforcement.* Drugs, flesh, poison, weapons– they themselves would know where best to find any product being sold in the dark hall. The man sighed and jammed a hand in his pocket, pulling out a pack of gum. He looked it over with a frown and popped one in his mouth, tossing the rest in a makeshift stall with a wink at the seller. *Let him pour over hours wondering what's so special about it*, he allowed the thought to bring him a dry chuckle.

Visibly relaxed now, he cleared his thoughts and covered the tattoo on his arm, lest it be discovered by someone who carried one of its counterparts. He'd thought about this evening too much to spend it in a petty black-market fight.

Ignoring the purrs of a woman offering him the finest opium and a merchant sporting priceless stolen jewels, he made his way to the guarded room on the other end, where once again a discreet flash of his ink admitted him within.

A flash of white greeted him on the other side. White tiles decked the room, save for the ceiling, which held a long mirror across the length of it. Across the table from him sat a red-faced man in a puff of smoke, cigar in one hand and a wicked blade in the other, a host of monitors beside him. Eye of The Market. He leaned forward with his mouth split in a grin, rivulets of sweat running down his temple into his short-cropped white hair.

"Welcome, my friend. Mr. Rahsut, I presume? I'm Gvadiskvi, we... spoke via our mutual contact, who sadly passed away today." He took his visitor's hand, shaking it and nodding. "Tragic, really, but you know how it is. I was hoping you'd stop by this week. Give us a chance to talk in person."

"Yes. A conversation has been long due." The man called Rahsut replied, pulling his hand back. He remained standing.

"Now, my friend. We are friends, yes? He-he. I would offer you a cigar, but unfortunately, I do not yet know if you are a friend. Let's save the cigar for later, then. A question for now. I heard from our friend Rihake you were taking an interest in the pits. You ask many questions, my friend, he-he. I must know, now, because I dislike having to answer so many questions, do you intend to partake in any way at all? Place a few bets, maybe indulge yourself in a match? Perhaps you'd like me to fix one for you, if only your first to get you a little start? He-he, say so, and we have a deal."

"I don't want to place bets, Gvadiskvi."

His host's eyes narrowed, his smile faltering "Then you will understand, there are steps to be taken. We must be cautious about our little venture, he-he."

"You misunderstand, *friend*." He spat with a smile of his own, "I wish to fight in the pits."

The red-faced man barked a laugh, hurling his cigar across the room. "Well, then, my friend, he-he, we must drink to that!" he shouted "I knew I liked you the moment you walked in." He poured out a strange green liquor in glass mugs kept behind his desk. "Come, Mr. Rahsut, we drink to victory. To living forever, and battering one's enemies to death!"

The man called Rahsut raked a hand through his dusty hair, clenching his fist at the drawn-out conversation "I do not drink before a fight. I will, however, take a whiff of your finest snow."

"Aye, it is a cold night, Mr. Rahsut, and you are a bold one." he sniggered "My new friend, a man of taste!"

The man called Gvadiskvi obliged, immediately sending for his finest of the drug. He invited his guest to sit across him and talk. "Come then, tell me." He grinned "What brings you here?"

Rahsut tilted his head, starting. "I t-"

"Huh-uh" he was cut off "Please, do not insult my intelligence. I'm curious," the other man leaned forward "I truly am. Why would a man like you resort to this?"

He stared across the table icily. "You don't know me. Don't pretend to."

"But surely someone such as you would have noticed the shadows trailing you, yes?" A giggle. "They've been watching you. The way you walk, the way you talk... the much-concealed desperation in your eyes... he-he."

"Maybe I have a death wish."

"Ah, but that's not the half of it, my dear Mr. Rahsut, is it?" his watery eyes gleamed, sending a shiver of revulsion down the addressed man's spine.

"Having a death wish doesn't have to be personal." He said quietly.

"Oh, but coming here always is."

His drug came and he consumed it, courtesy of the House. He rolled his neck, grasping at his colliding thoughts and the clarity he now had. He pulled out the battered old pocket watch; A half hour still remained before he'd fight. The man called Rahsut suddenly realized that he was talking and stopped, visibly shaken.

He found himself staring across at his half-witless host who beseeched him to continue.

"You were at the bit where you had the epiphany after giving up your old ways, when the fighting was over. Go on, then."

He considered for a moment, then shrugged. *No harm done. Screw it, it wouldn't matter after tonight anyway.*

"When it struck me," he spoke through the piece of gum still in his mouth "How much the stars and I are alike.

Gvadiskvi hummed in appreciation "How poetic for a man of your... bearing. But do tell, how so?"

"It's silly, really, but also true." he snorted a scoff, waving his hand airily. "When they die, it's got to be a cosmic carnage, or no one knows cares, because otherwise no one would know when they die."

The other man spoke through a puff of smoke as he lit another cigar "Ah, much like battle veterans and mercenaries such as yourself, eh? He-he."

"Yes, and the natural way is... too mundane." He tasted the word on his tongue, and how morbid it felt. "So, I thought why not die in a carnage and make people care."

"Care?" Gvadiskvi went silent for a long moment. "Do you truthfully think the people he-"

"Enough to place bets, anyway." He retorted.

The elder man undid a button on his shirt, rolling back his shoulders. "Fair enough. You want to bring business to me, who am I to refuse, my violent friend?"

A bolt of lightning went up his spine, and Rahsut tilted his head. His host noticed it.

"Oh, come on. I've been running the pits for nine years now, how many of your kind do you think I've seen?" he huffed a laugh, thick smoke momentarily covering his face. "I lost the count from not caring, Mr. Rahsut, if I ever was honest, and you're simply another face in that pile. Men like you, you only like violence. Do you know why?"

He looked at him, very still.

"Because it's the easiest thing to do." He continued, twirling the knife in his hand. "So you go about your life, with violence as your creed, until suddenly one day you realize that you're all alone. So, what do you do?

He said nothing as the eyes across his bore into his own with a cruel smile.

"You turn on yourself, becoming violent to life itself. Hating your existence, and desperate for the bittersweet mercy the *idea* of death offers." Gvadiskvi looked into his eyes. "And so...

94

"You turn to men like me. Like I said, Mr. Rahsut, I recognize people like you. I think you'll find some kindred spirits in here this evening. Try to be merciful to them a little, he-he." He finished with a twinkle in his eyes.

Feeling uncomfortably vulnerable, he rode on a surge of blood and vaulted over the table in a blur, grabbing Gvadiskvi to whirl behind him, the knife now in his hand and held to his host. "If you claim to know my motivations so well, then tell me, *friend*," he spat, "Why don't I be a gentleman and grant you some mercy right now?"

The man laughed softly, feeling his own blade digging into his throat. "I am trying to be polite, Mr. Rahsut, but if you move that knife one inch closer to me, I will rip your heart out. Besides, we both know that you'd rather put on an impressive display, if you are so adamant on dying."

Rahsut released him, taking a step back. "The pits are crowded tonight," Gvadiskvi remarked with the eyes of a predator "Our old friend Rihake picked you a good night to fight, he-he..."

The fighting pits had been emptied and a large area cleared for the closing event of the night. It was sparsely decorated, a handful of oil drums scattered to provide cover and a few low-hanging bulbs as the only source of light in the wide hall.

The crowd was brimming with nervous energy, with people shoving each other for the best spot to view the last fight without falling inside. Rules of the arena were clear; A single step in and you were fair game.

The audience silently parted as its supreme benefactor glided through. Aytanpar Gvadiskvi, the man who ran the pits, and every piece of low-life scum that haunted the mines. He raised his arm, holding a glass of exquisite liquor, and the world fell silent.

"Greetings, Children of the Pits!" he boomed "I have a special night in store for you. The matches till now have offered but a slice of the excitement to come." He looked at those who would fight now, spotting them in the audience.

"No-life is better than half a life. Tonight, the six individuals gathered in the arena share more than blood-brothers do in a lifetime! They share this thought, and are willing to fight to the death to prove it. They are the superior people amongst us, for these men and women have looked into the eyes of desire and stared it down. Riches or luxury, a good, quiet life... that's too much to ask of them. They live for the combat, and for the combat they willingly die! Most of them, anyway..." he trailed off.

The crowd cheered. The man nodded and continued, "We are graced with our weapons master, Mr. Black, offering us the chance to witness his latest wares in action!"

The crowd went wild, shrieks and whoops filling the air as the said man joined Gvadiskvi, completely decked in black, only parts of his face not covered by his wide-brimmed hat or sunglasses visible as his lip burst in a cheery laugh. He waved. "Tonight, I bring to you," he started in a deep voice as the crowd went silent "The only functioning prototypes of my latest gun, a tranquilizer coated with poison from deadly toads... and from my herb garden. Highly flammable, although one wouldn't need fire for them to do their job. A slight graze could end a grizzly's life, to say nothing of our own. Up for auction next week!"

Murmurs streaked across the room as Gvadiskvi continued, "To make it more of a challenge, each of the fighters are equipped with a gun, good for two shots. No other weapons. Look closely, for if you blink, you may miss it... but mind your eyes, he-he."

At a signal, six figures stepped in the cleared area. A lithe figure prowled in, carefully eyeing her opponents. The woman had a vicious smile plastered on her face, tracing a finger up her leather-like body armor. "My new guns will go well with the gear."

The other woman grunted and flicked her the finger. A thin man slicked a tongue over his teeth, filed into sharp fangs. "We'll see about that, doll." Two other men staggered inside, either drunk or badly beaten up recently.

Rahsut was handed his gun as he weighed his options. Oil drums for cover. Low-hanging lightbulbs. A stale piece of gum in his mouth and a gun with two rounds of poison within. He nodded, taking a deep breath. *In mortality lies my victory. In victory, a worthy death. Till my last breath, the carnage will not stop.* He looked up in front of him. The carnage must stop. Tonight, then. *Death is life.*

A bell rang without warning and the crowd roared as slivers of crimson flew all around, spraying up a shower of blood where they struck. He moved in a flash, ducking past a couple of darts and backhanding a lightbulb. Those nearest to him flinched, momentarily blinded.

Those two died first.

He shimmied up behind the loudmouthed girl with the protective gear, swiftly shooting at the unbalanced man across the room. He was dead before he fell, the dart buried in his eye. Grabbing her by the hair, he smashed her nose on the oil drum and she cried out, instinctively raising a hand to her face. He snaked a hand into the side of her neck and snapped, snatching the gun out of her hands even as her body fell.

He ducked as a barrage of darts flew past him. Pressing his back against a drum, Rahsut peeked to find the other drunk-or-injured man already dead while the man with the razor-sharp teeth wrestled with the bulky woman, their guns tossed a few feet away.

Huh. So much for that momentary truce.

He spied the lightbulb near him, still swinging. He grabbed it with one hand, pulling out the chewing gum with the other and sticking it on the bulb, recoiling when the hot glass burned his finger.

At least this will go quicker than I anticipated, he thought as the glowing bulb twinkled like the stars outside. *Damned twinkler.*

He moved quickly, moving behind another oil drum as he fired twice at the one directly beneath the bulb, then tossed the dead girl's now empty gun at it for good measure. A thin spray or oil spurted from it, steadily growing into a tiny fountain leaking oil that quickly spread across the floor.

This caught the attention of the woman, who had finished crushing the throat of the thin man and pummeling him to death with her fists. She grinned, going for the two guns at her feet even as he leaped, and the world froze.

In that moment, Rahsut saw everything. The horror on Gvadiskvi's face, the victory on the woman's, the final moments of the mine as he shot at the lightbulb which burst apart, flames engulfing the oil an-

Boom.

The next day, all the papers talked about the mine blow-up. A gas explosion, they called it. The official report said that no one was around when it happened, no one got hurt. The clean-up crew moved quickly, doing multiple sweeps and gathering what they found before loading the bodies in a truck to be taken away and incinerated. Yet no one noticed a single hand twitching still, of the dead man who would still live, outliving his own carnage. No one noticed the mouth speak obscenities in broken whispers, cursing at himself, at the stars, and at life itself.

THE END

Aunt Delia

Tommy Noris

"Julia dear, come quick! Your breakfast is getting cold." Anne stood straight as though there was a ruler in her back, her dark, opal blue eyes glimmering. She set down a stacked plate of four golden pancakes paired with fruits and syrup as her sister cascaded down the stairs. She, too, was standing tall and straight and had blue eyes, though hers were somewhat lighter in color. They both inherited that feature from their parents, who had died in a motorcar crash. Now it was just them, their older brother George, and their Aunt Delia.

"I'm here now," she said as she took a seat at the dining table. "Good morning." She said, glancing at each member with an artificial smile plastered to her face. It was a reflex they had all built over the years. Oddly enough, today, their Aunt wasn't like that. She seemed to be anxious, her thin shoulders a bit hunched. The family began to neatly and quietly eat their meals until a resounding knock on their front door made Delia jump, the clattering of her fork reverberating against the cream tiled floor.

George rose from his chair and, picking up his aunt's stray utensil, said, "I'll get the door," and walked across their living room, opening the door to a man in a light coffee-colored sweater vest and a matching hat atop his graying head.

"Good morning, sir. What can I do for you?" George inquired at the man, smiling.

He hesitated. "I work at Edgewood State Hospital, and I am upset to inform you that... your grandmother passed late last afternoon. She was incredibly ill. I'm sorry."

"My... grandmother?" George still bore the same feigned smile, but rather, with a trace of confusion.

"Yes," the man responded, his voice soaked in sympathy. "She was overcome with a terminal illness and battled for so many months." He took the hat off and held it in his hands, head hung down, so that his thin, gray hairs were exposed, shining like silver in the sunlight. "We shall give you and your family time to grieve, but know that she left you an inheritance in her will. Two hundred dollars each. You may go to the bank soon and collect it if you'd like." There was a pause, and the man bid George farewell, leaving him alone at the doorstep.

"Who was there? Come back inside George, it's getting much too warm for you to stay out in the sun for too long." Anne demanded softly.

George shut the door, perplexed, but still maintained his smile. "Oh, it wasn't anything of importance. Just a man coming to announce some news."

"What news would there be to tell us?" Aunt Delia asked, fidgeting with her pearl necklace.

He was hesitant to speak and kept pausing to gulp as if there was a piece of food wedged in his throat. "Well, you see... our... *grandmother* passed away. The man told me that we had gotten some sort of inheritance. We each have two hundred dollars."

"Grandmother? Why, you don't have a grandmother, darling. Come now, sit and finish your food." Aunt Delia responded rather quickly and laughed, but one of unease.

They consumed the rest of their breakfast in silence, the warm, luminescent sunlight filling their entire mansion.

"George, I think you ought to go and collect the inheritance at the bank soon," Aunt Delia said the following day.

"Auntie, please, don't be so naive," Anne interjected. She walked over to stand in front of her aunt, her hands perched on her hips.

"the man could have been lying to us. It could be a fraud, and you had said it yourself, we don't have a grandmother!"

Her aunt kneeled to her niece's height and grasped her shoulders sweetly, her voice coated in honey. "Darling, listen to me. I understand why you are skeptical, for you always are, but is there any harm in trying?"

"There could be," Anne maintained a firm look, but her words softened, unfazed by her aunt's typical method of sugarcoating her words to manipulate. "You'd best not go, George. It's dangerous."

"George-"

"Alright, Aunt Delia, I'll go early tomorrow morning if you two would just stop fighting!" George interrupted as the pair settled down. "But if I sense something is wrong like Anne says, I'll go straight home."

—

When George arrived at the bank the next morning, it was half-past nine.

"Good morning, sir," he said to a man wearing a light blue shirt at the front desk. He ripped a sheet of paper from the checkbook and filled out his required information. Once he had finished, he handed it to the man.

104

He scanned the slip of paper and in return, gave George a typewritten record of his aunt's account history.

George's brows furrowed as he traveled down the list. *Odd,* he thought, *no one's made a recent deposit.*

Seeing as there was no use in going to the bank, George went home, meeting Anne at the door.

"Did you find anything?"

"There was nothing. You were right."

She whirled around to face her aunt. "See? The man lied."

Delia sighed and walked away. "Okay, darling, you were right."

Julia waited until her aunt had left the room to pull both siblings together. "What if Aunt Delia is hiding something from us?"

Anne rolled her eyes at her sister. "Don't be silly, Julia."

"Well, I think we should consider it."

"Oh, please, our aunt isn't a madman," Anne replied with an accusatory tone.

"But what if she is? When George told us about... the grandmother, she seemed nervous! Is that not strange to you?"

"Stop it," George mumbled. He hated fights.

Anne paused, ignoring her brother's request. "Well, *I think* we should trust our Aunt," she said forcefully.

Julia scoffed. "Alright, if you won't hear my opinion, I'll find out by myself!" She stormed off to her aunt's bedroom.

—

Why won't they let me have a say? My ideas are just as good as anyone else's. She thought as she closed the bedroom door, careful not to make a sound.

She sat down on her aunt's bed. *I don't need them. I'll find what our aunt is hiding by myself.*

She sat idly for a minute and scanned the room until she laid eyes on the closet. She rummaged through her aunt's things but found nothing that could have been used as evidence there. She searched underneath her bed, in her vanity and her dresser, but found nothing.

Julia sighed and sat on the bed. *I've been searching for thirty minutes, yet I've found nothing. Anne was right again.* She was beginning to exit the room to tell Anne she had given up when she heard a small *creak* from one of the floorboards.

Julia paused. She managed to find it: the board had been marked with a thin scrape in the wood. She pried it open with a screwdriver she had found in her aunt's drawers.

—

106

Why is Julia taking so long? Anne thought as she talked with her aunt to stop her from heading to her room. *If Auntie goes upstairs, Julia's going to be in trouble. Oh, please, hurry up, Julia! I can't keep this up any longer!*

"George, why don't you go upstairs to check on Julia? I think she's in her room." She said, turning to her brother anxiously.

Understanding his sister's appeal, he replied, "Of course, I'll call her down for dinner," and went to Delia's room.

"Julia, come downstairs. Dinner is ready," he said, opening the door.

Julia was kneeling on the floor, a sheet of paper in her hand. "It's... a will," she said quietly.

George shut the door and kneeled beside her. "Our grandmother's will?"

"I suppose so," she replied, her eyes glued to her name, next to it, the number two hundred.

"Two hundred dollars..." George murmured, revisiting his conversation with the man two days prior. "We should tell Anne. Later, of course," he added nimbly.

"Yes, perhaps when Auntie goes to sleep. I'm keeping this for now." Julia replied, her voice dull.

"Hurry," the pair heard Anne shout from the floor below. "your food is getting cold,"

They quickly replaced the floorboard and rushed downstairs to eat their dinner.

—

"Anne!" George whispered from Julia's bedroom, an oil lamp illuminated at her desk. "Come here, make sure that Auntie is asleep."

"What's wrong?" She asked, walking over to stand in front of her siblings. She paused as she realized what had happened. "Julia, you found something, didn't you?"

Her sister nodded lamentably. "George and I think we found our grandmother's will."

Anne took the paper, scanning it underneath the glow of the lamp. She noticed faint writing on the opposite side and turned it over. She grew pale and stiffened. "Look at this..." she said, feeling as if all the air had escaped from her lungs.

"Kill Delia Robinson," Julia read aloud. She faltered and emitted a short cry, putting her hand over her mouth.

"That's why... that's why she hid it," George swallowed.

"We shouldn't do this anymore. Please, just put it away and forget it ever happened-" Julia pleaded, her lips quivering.

"No."

"No? George, are you insane?" Anne hissed, her expression distorted.

"I'll explain later, just get some rest. Please."

Anne and George headed to their rooms without a word when they heard a thud coming from their aunt's room that made the two stop in their tracks.

Their aunt emerged from her bedroom, holding what seemed to be a knife in hand.

The children's chests contracted, their hearts pounding like the fast beat of a drum.

"You... you found it," Delia staggered across the hall. "I'm so sorry that I have to do this, children, I truly am. If only you hadn't found the damn will," She was aggressive; they had never seen her in such a state. She stepped towards George. "I love you, darling," she said, but it wasn't sweet.

Towering over her nephew, she raised her arm, but a small gasp left her body. She fell limp to the ground, Julia holding the screwdriver she used to open the floorboards.

There was a long moment of silence. "What did I do...?" Julia whimpered. "Auntie, I'm so sorry..." The screwdriver fell from her hands, and she fainted next to the body that lay dormant on the ground.

THE END

The Unplanned

Mathias Olsson

A man sat in a dark room, alone. He faced a wall, a wall of Screens. Each about a foot squared in size, every single one showing a different picture. There were hundreds, maybe thousands. The man, Khan, glanced over the Screens, seeming to analyze each one in that brief instant.

Khan turned away from the Screens and opened a drawer. Every single citizen had a file. He knew them all. Flipping through the people, Khan stopped at a certain page and removed it from the rest.

This certain sheet was worn and the picture faded. Obviously a certain point of interest. Frowning slightly, Khan looked back up at the Screens. After decades of practice, he had no trouble searching through the hundreds of cameras and spotting his man. A younger guy, a bit shifty.

Khan's cameras showed every nook and cranny of his 'perfect empire.' Every alley, every street, every room, every person. Nothing escaped his attention. The Khan saw all.

111

And now, he saw the young man shuffling around, near the outer wall. A wary glance around him, the kid snuck into a shop, disappearing from view. Khan looked to another Screen. It showed the guy entering and then sneaking to the back. It was only the briefest movement, but Khan caught it. The young man stole something. Quickly, he departed.

Shoplifting wasn't a big deal in his opinion, but it was the worst crime anyone could commit in the Oasis. Khan had sculpted and shaped his society so well, that stealing was the biggest offense, nothing more. And Khan dealt out punishment- hard.

Khan sighed. *Fool.* He thought, powering off the Screens for the time being. *Don't you realize how good you have it here? How good I've written it all?* But Khan was hardly surprised. Everything in the algorithms told of what the kid was planning to do. Every single moment was carefully choreographed, almost of a map to the future. The Khan knew all.

And now, the man touched a smooth panel on his desk and closed his eyes. *:Bring citizen #0048027 to the Deck. Crime of shoplifting and requires immediate attention.:* The message was broadcasted through the minds of every Keeper in the Sector. Khan knew the young man would be down in the Deck, in less than five minutes. Still, he allowed himself to take his time.

Khan had named his city the Oasis. Fitting name, too. It had the only water for hundreds of miles around. Or so he said. It was the only city known to be left in existence. Or so he told them. The Khan was a crafty man, unknowing if even his own abilities.

While the city was perfect and beautiful on the inside, the surrounding area was its opposite. The eye was met with red, red, and more red. Red earth, red sky, red air, red everything. Even the raging fires in the distance were red. That was the result of the Cataclysm; the disaster which tipped the world on its very head.

So Khan had created this perfect city, attending to the people's needs and wants. They were simple, and pleased easily. Exactly how he had intended them to be. Exactly how the algorithm had shown it. The people wanted their history, Khan had given them history. Only, he was the author. The entire book was a farce, a fairytale. Life was never that perfect. But it was going to be now. They had wanted protection, Khan had given them the city. Every day, he even broadcasted updates on the attempts to beat back the raging fires around them.

Everything they knew was because of him. Khan chuckled softly; a chilling sound. He had created the community with his own two hands, weeding out the undesired people and knowledge. He had programmed the algorithm to predict every move the people would make. He had every aspect covered. For his people's benefit, Khan had sheltered them from what they used to be, and created them anew.

Although seven minutes had gone by, Khan let the young man wait a little longer. Almost from nowhere, he produced a Key, the small black box that held captive his secrets. Khan locked the door. He moved to the far wall, his steps quiet but sure. Silently, he touched the Key to a specific point, and a panel opened. Khan pulled out an object, bigger than most of its kind. A Circuit. Another careful glance at the door before the button.

The thing lit up. Khan exhaled softly, and read the message on the face of the Circuit. "You can't fool them forever." It read. "Someday, they'll find out about you; about your city; about the fires. Everything. It's all fake. You can't keep up the facade forever . . ."

Khan chuckled. *Oh I can. He thought. They're too blind to see. They'll never know.* The leader looked up, his eyes blazing. In that same instant, the room went dark . . .

And suddenly, Khan found himself falling. Falling into a chasm. An abyss. One with no bottom. A dream or reality? Whatever it was, this had not been calculated. This was not part of the algorithm.

Khan hit the ground with an impact to kill, yet he felt no pain. Terrified of the unplanned, the unknown, he opened his eyes.

Green. All he could see was green. Green to rival the red of the past. Green to pain his eyes.

The Khan squinted in the bright sunlight, a soft yellow glow, much unlike the sun of the past.

This was a new place. *This* was the land beyond the flames. *This* was what he had feared for decades.

Khan shut his eyes to mask the turmoil inside. This was *exactly* what he had dedicated his life to terminating.

Suddenly, the man found himself once again in the dark room. Slowly his eyes adjusted to the dim of it all. Oh his face, pure terror was shown.

Almost as if controlled by some other force, he found himself moving across the room. The Khan shell lifted its arm to another wall, holding another Key in hand—inside Khan was fighting himself to break out of the trance.

As if by magic, the body disobeyed it's master and opened the secret panel. Inside, a glowing red button resided.

The real Khan fought against his body, willing it not to go ahead with it . . . But it did.

The uncontrollable hand reached out and firmly pressed the button. A second later, a siren began to blare.

All Khan's Screens shut off but one. Finally able to control himself once again, the leader rushed to it. Pictured on the Screen was a fiery wall of blazing flames.

All at once, it was gone. The flames disappeared and the world beyond was revealed. Green. All he could see was green. With a howl, Khan threw himself into a mad rage, blinded by his own terror.

This was not in the algorithm. And now only the known was unknown . . .

THE END

My Father's Voice

Ray Dyer

The sun wore a ten-foot smile that could have been drawn with a licorice Mr. Sketch Scented Marker. It rose majestically over an aerial shot of endless pines, the original "Penn's Woods," needles glossed amber by the nascent light of morning. Lettering proclaimed, *THE BEATING HEART OF AMERICA.* Sandra glanced from the billboard to the wilderness surrounding her and asked aloud, "Who puts a billboard full of trees in the middle of a forest?"

She'd begun asking questions of the universe about two hours earlier, when it had occurred to her that the only living things she had seen since her gas-station lunch had been cows grazing in the few places where the earth glimpsed the sky.

"There should be one of those signs like you see in the desert," she told the speedometer wryly. "Last gas for two hundred miles."

A minute passed.

She said, "You *did* say that you wanted to get away from the kids for awhile."

Sandra rolled her eyes and ceded this round to herself. She had said those very words. She needed an escape from the kids, but moreso from the judgmental parents and the administration that sided with them. Just, nobody wanted to hear that. A teacher who needed to get away from the kids was something everyone thought they understood, because they wanted time away from their kids, too. So, Sandra had taken the path of least resistance, unaware that a letter would arrive within an hour to announce the death of the father she never knew and summon her to Middle of Nowhere, Pennsylvania.

Even the GPS lady had given up fifty miles ago. After a few minutes of intermittent recalculation, she had just quit the trip without so much as a good-bye.

"And good riddance to you," Sandra said. Her voice fell flat. She couldn't even manage an echo for company. Worse, she had finished eleven of the twelve cans of Mountain Dew that she had brought along for the trip. Gas stations only sold bottles, which made the soda taste like plastic. It had been a long trip here, but the trip home promised to be both long and dry.

Her questions all played out to no resolution. *Who was he? How did he die? Why had he included her in his will after letting her grow up without knowing him?* And, yes, *What did the letter mean about claiming an inheritance?*

The most important of those questions would go unanswered forever. Mom proved a dead end not worth pursuing. She had never spoken his name and forbade Sandra from even mentioning him. And on the rare occasions in the past when teenaged Sandy had thrown caution to the wind and forced the subject, Mom crushed the subject with a manic light in her eyes that Sandra recognized as fear. Fear of a man who had disappeared before his daughter was born and never returned.

The GPS woke up to declare, "Turn right, and your destination is on your right," words Sandra nearly missed due to her yelp of terror, born partly of surprise but also of the memory of that light in her mother's eyes.

"On your right," turned out to be a subjective statement. Perhaps the property had belonged to Sandra's father, but the unpaved road she now traveled showed no sign of habitation. In fact, the trees hugged the road so tightly that she lost the sun beneath twining branches. She carried on this way for the better part of a mile, countless divots and rocks battering her worn shocks as the GPS lady slipped back into a well-deserved coma, before abruptly reaching a clearing that would have been right at home in a documentary on the English aristocracy.

119

"More like 'The Fall of the House of Usher,'" Sandra said. Her foot came off the gas. She let the car idle ahead, all the old questions replaying in her mind. *Who the hell did Mom marry?*

On the third floor several windows were broken. No curtains hung there, only darkness. Once as a college sophomore, Sandra had imagined herself a writer rather than a teacher. She had submitted her finest haunted house story as her final project in The American Short Story. She'd passed, but the professor bled comments onto every page. She could still visualize the handwritten note that followed the first paragraph – "Never refer to windows as eyes...*TRITE.*"

"Fuck you, Dr. Fultz," Sandra said now. "This bitch is staring right at me."

The car came to a halt and she got out, gripping her last Mountain Dew like a child with a blanket. No one awaited her arrival. She saw no indication that anyone had been here in some time. The grass stood almost to her knees, and the upstairs windows weren't the only thing in need of maintenance.

"Leave behind what is familiar and comfortable," Sandra said, quoting the letter from her father's attorney. She stared back at the house. "I am so far beyond familiar and comfortable right now."

She hesitated. She knew all the reasons to turn back. The shadows deepened among the trees at the edges of the clearing. The dilapidated mansion loomed. She was keenly aware of the fact that even the nearest stranger lived fifty miles away. No one knew she had come. Most of all, she couldn't banish the memory of the panic in Mom's eyes whenever she mentioned her father.

In the end, her litany of questions overruled the roster of concerns. The questions repeated in her mind with no resolution to be found, and she knew they would never be silenced if she gave up this opportunity to answer even one of them. Sandra climbed the steps.

The door was locked, but a moment after she tried the knob, a panel fell open at about waist-height in the wall next to where she stood. It opened with a metallic clang and revealed a slot wide enough to slip most of her hand through. Etched into wood above the opening were five letters: PHONE.

Sandra stared.

"You can't be serious."

Her words returned faintly from the edge of the clearing. The echo she had craved not long ago now served to reinforced how alone she was. She frowned.

The voice telling her to go home repeated the roster of concerns. It used Mom's voice.

The other voice repeated the litany of questions. It sounded like Sandra. They were *her* questions, and all her reasons to leave belonged to a woman who lived in fear two hundred miles north of here.

"I'm trusting you, Dad."

Sandra slipped her phone into the slot. It landed on something just beyond her view, then slowly disappeared into the house as if conveyed by unseen hands. A mechanical hum commenced, and the metal cover rose steadily to cover the opening. Then, two more sounds, one ominous, the other frightening. The crunch of plastic, glass, and steel from somewhere just out of sight. An audible click as the door lock disengaged.

Sandra jerked door open and leapt inside, ignoring the interior as she scanned the floor for her phone. It lay in a heap, screen shattered, compressed to half its normal thickness, twisted circuit board exposed.

"Son of a bitch," she gasped, and the difference in the sound of her voice drew her attention upward and inside the house. Lit by ebbing sunlight, the foyer opened into a long corridor. Steps curved to a landing. On the right, a parlor. Left, the dining room.

Archways led farther in each direction. The door swung shut behind her, its lock clicking shut.

Her fight was short-lived. She couldn't break the front door, but the downstairs possessed many ornate windows she would be sad—but not unwilling—to break. A locked door was ominous, but she was no more trapped now than she had been when the door hung open. Steeling her nerves, she began an investigation, moving fast because her only flashlight was now so much shatterproof glass and mangled electronics on the floor.

There was no note, or anything addressed to her. Sandra found just two things of interest. A broken window along the west side of the house would save her the trouble of breaking glass. Also, one door beneath the steps had no handle but she suspected would open if she stepped even farther away from what felt *familiar and comfortable.*

"Screw it," Sandra said. "My dad was Jigsaw. That's all I need to know."

She walked to the broken window and swung a leg into open air. She froze, straddling the sill, when a man's voice broke the silence. "Sandy."

Her name.

His voice.

"Dearest Sandy. You are free to leave. But, if you do, this will be the last time you hear my voice."

She stared into the house as he spoke, looking for the speakers, but it was late enough that his voice could have projected from a soundbar directly over her head and she wouldn't have been able to see it. Everything more than a few feet from a window lay draped in shadow. Worse, as Sandra considered the yard—rather, the *grounds*—her father's words took on an alternate, darker meaning.

"Last time I hear your voice," Sandra said softly. Sitting there, half in and half out of the broken window, she did not feel like she was on the edge of escape so much as she felt exposed. The pools of darkness between the distant trees did not feel empty as they had when she first arrived. Sandra found that she could not dispel the sense that there were eyes on her, waiting for her to make a choice. Maybe her final one.

Shaking her head, Sandra swung her leg inside. She dropped to the floor and hurried before the last of the light could dip below the horizon. Eyes narrowed, she studied the contraption mounted next to the door with no knob, a wooden tube roughly the size and shape of a can koozie. Considerable work had gone into burning the image of the Mountain Dew logo into the surface of the wood.

124

"I get it" Sandra muttered, "you stalked me." She lifted the can and attempted to slide it into the koozie. The bottom of the can came down across the top. The can and the tube weren't just similarly sized. They were exactly the same size.

"You can't be serious."

She bit her lip, keeping the best of her curses—a tirade that would have impressed her most jaded students—inside for now. She popped the can open, listening to the divine release of carbonation, inhaling the slightly fruity aroma, and then she poured it into the replica container on the wall. As the last drop fell, a subtle click triggered within the wall. The door swung open, not slowly but all at once, and Sandra found herself swaying above a steep flight of steps. The bottom few were lit by a pale blue light.

"Oh, hell no."

And yet, once again, the litany of questions. *Who was he? How did he die?* Had *he died?*

Who was among the trees?

Sandra ran a hand along the wall as she descended the steps. She studied the blue light every step of the way, ready to race to the top and out the open window if she caught any glimpse of movement. At the same time, she dreaded the sound of the door slamming shut behind her so much that she had to fight against closing her eyes in anticipation. Throughout her descent, the glow remained steady. Nothing moved. The door never closed.

Her foot came down on the basement floor. Ahead stretched a room with damp stone walls. A bare bulb, hung at the end of a sturdy chain. Beneath the light, on a stone dais, rested a lacquered coffin. Atop it sat a framed photograph. Sandra hurried toward it without hesitation, eager to see the faces before her. A door she had not noticed swung shut behind her.

A roar she felt as much as heard. Some beast had been let loose, but it was one with no mouth. Water flowed in torrents through a dozen corrugated pipes set mid-way on the walls. The mildew smell of a stagnant lake filled the air. The blue light, knocked askew by tremors shaking the foundation, swung overhead, creating mad shadows. Sandra saw dark shapes flop out of the pipes; some were certainly frogs, but others were longer, sinuous.

"Jesus!" Sandra cried, partly from horror but also no small amount of disbelief.

"Dearest Sandy," her father's voice—she never doubted it was him—said again, barely audible above the cacophony. The water had already reached her ankles. It was *cold.*

"Dad?"

126

"What inheritance did you expect to find?"

His voice emanated from everywhere and nowhere. She raced into the room, not bothering with the door, looking for any exit that might have been invisible at a distance. There were no windows, she had entered through the only door. As the water reached her knees she leaned against the wall farthest from one of the spewing pipes and swiped at her tears with shaking hands.

"I don't know," she said. "I didn't come here for *things.*"

The voice was spent. Again, she realized that his words possessed a double-meaning. She had mistaken a statement for a question, but the sadistic bastard had been gloating. *Well? I left before you were even a baby. Your mother made it pretty damn clear that I wasn't a good person. What did you expect?*

Sandra screamed. The water had risen to her waist. She splashed her fists angrily in the water, spraying the few parts of herself that she had managed to keep dry.

"I just wanted to know who you were!" she cried. Her legs threatened to buckle. She wanted to curl into a ball and sob, but any chance for that was long gone. She missed her kids. Something brushed against her leg for the first time. It bent around her, a lover's caress, then was gone.

The voice returned, almost inaudible now that the water's fury roiled at the level of her ears. "Then come join me."

Sandra stared at the coffin and the picture still atop it. From here she could see a young man next to a woman who looked like— that was Mom! And in the man's arms was cradled a little girl in a yellow dress.

"I remember that dress," Sandra said, no longer caring that she could not hear her own words.

On shaky legs she dragged herself to the dais. She stared at the smiling couple and their child. Mom looked like any proud mother posing for a family picture. Baby Sandra had a smile fit to brighten the whole world. She did not know the man holding her, but she recognized the house looming behind them. Voiceless, she mouthed her confusion as she stared at her mother's smiling face.

"We were here."

Sandra cried out, swiping the framed picture from the coffin's lacquered surface and gripping the lid before her nerve could fail. She threw the lid open and stared down on the man within. It was the man in the picture, grown old. Whatever had taken his life had withered him in the process. His eyes were closed.

"Is this unfamiliar and uncomfortable enough for you, Daddy?" she shrieked.

128

The water poured in. If anything, the flow had increased as time went on.

Sandra stared into the coffin and the frail remains unable to fill the narrow space. She knew what he intended for her to do. She waited till the water froze the bottoms of her breasts before clambering inside. Her hands came down on his chest and she jerked away as if burned. Inside his fine suit he was nothing more than bones and parchment flesh. His head turned to face her in a crackling of vertebrae, and for a moment she was sure his eyes would open—and then she would surrender to this madness, just check out and float away. They remained closed.

The water rose. Soon it would spill over the coffin walls. Sandra glanced up at the coffin lid, the grim realization of how this would need to end, sealed inside with the man who hadn't disappeared quite so long ago as she had been led to believe. Except now she saw another message. Four letters scrawled across the bottom of the light—as if by a Mr. Sketch Scented Marker—PULL.

Desperately, Sandra reached up from the coffin and took hold of the chain above the light. She pulled. The chain descended easily, the bulb coming to rest on her father's chest. At once, the water stopped flowing. The door at the base of the steps rose, lifted into the ceiling among sounds of pulleys and chains.

"Dearest Sandy," her father said. "Your mother sought to keep you from me, but I was never far. She has many justified regrets, but one thing that we have always agreed upon was you. You were our marvel. Our perfect addition to this world."

"Thanks, Dad," Sandra whispered, easing herself out of the coffin. She found that the words were not entirely insincere. The noise of the drains rose to a drone that rivaled the thunder that had just ended. She spoke to him anyway. "But you never answered my question. Who the hell were you?"

"I was not a good man," her father said, and for the first time Sandra felt certain that there were no speakers in the house, not even hidden ones.

She stared into the swaying shadows. The unseen serpent writhed once more around her leg, but it had nothing to do with the way she could feel each individual hair on her body standing in unison.

"Come upstairs, dear Sandy. I may not be a part of this world any longer, but we have your inheritance to discuss."

THE END

Ex

Stephanie Anne

"What do you think?"

"What do I think of what?"

"Well, it's sad, isn't it?"

She stared for a moment at the scene in front of her, not really feeling any particularly strong emotions one way or the other.

"I suppose it is."

"And I think it's scary."

"Oh yeah?" she asked nonchalantly.

Her co-worker nodded. "That could have been one of us."

She shrugged. "Probably not."

"But what if it had been you or me here working late instead of Jen?"

She looked back at their manager's body, lying a few feet away behind police tape. There was blood everywhere, and a knife was sticking out of her chest.

"No, she was stabbed a lot. I don't think this was random."

131

"Oh! You think it might be Jen's ex?"

She simply shrugged.

They waited in silence, off to the side, for the police to question them. While they waited, she watched as the body was examined. The knife was dusted for fingerprints, but it didn't look like any were found. She was almost surprised by that.

By the time they took the body away, there was someone questioning her co-worker. Now that the body was gone, she watched them instead. Her co-worker was a blubbering mess. The police officer remained calm. She supposed he was attractive, but that didn't really mean anything. She found it very easy to find other people attractive, and was the victim of frequent crushes. The last one had not ended well for her. She had confessed her feelings too soon and had been rejected. She told herself not to fall for the police officer.

But, when he finished questioning her co-worker and began to move towards her, she could feel another crush coming on.

"Morning. I'm Detective Wellington," he said with a warm smile. She knew instantly that she was doomed.

"Morning," she said as coldly as she could. She didn't want to seem to interested or too desperate. That's usually what drove people away: the reek of desperation and loneliness that hung

132

about her like a perfume. But she was also very good at being cold and detached. That was her baseline when she wasn't falling head over heels in love.

"You were the second employee to arrive this morning, correct?"

"Yeah, I stayed late to help close up last night, so I was a little late getting here this morning. By the time I got in," she said, nodding to her co-worker, "the police had already been called."

"So, you were here last night? With Jen? You might have been the last person to see her then."

"Maybe," she shrugged. "I guess. I left first, so I don't know if anyone came in after."

"Your colleague mentioned an abusive ex. Do you think he would have come by?"

"Who knows. Jen told me she had been thinking of going back to him. I told her it was a mistake."

"I see."

Detective Wellington asked her a few more questions about their workplace environment, Jen's relationships with her employees and her ex. She tried to answer as best she could, but she kept getting distracted. She kept getting lost in his eyes.

"Well, this has been a lot for you to deal with this morning," the detective said eventually as he slipped his notebook into his pocket and took out a card. "If you think of anything else, please call me."

When he said that, her normally still heart skipped a beat.

~ ~ ~

Work had been closed down for a couple of days while the crime scene was cleaned up. She spent much of that time sitting around her apartment, starring at the card Detective Wellington had given her. She kept wracking her brain, trying to come up with reasons to call him. She couldn't think of anything else about Jen that would be useful to him. By the time her workplace reopened, she had an idea. She used her last heartbreak as inspiration; but this time, she was determined that things would work out in her favour.

After closing, she waited until she was the last one left before making the call. She was a horrible actress, and an even worse liar, but she tried her best to sound scared when Detective Wellington answered the phone.

"I'm just scared that what happened to Jen will happen to me," she said, trying to make her voice tremble after he had tried to calm her down. "Can you please come and stay with me while I close up. You don't even have to come inside. You can just wait by the door. Please. Please!"

134

"Okay. Okay. Try to stay calm. Take a deep breath. I'll..." he sighed. "I guess I can be there in... five minutes. Are you going to be okay to wait that long until I get there?"

"I think so."

When he arrived, she immediately opened the door for him before he could decide whether to wait outside or not. She wanted him to be close.

"Thank you so much."

"You're welcome. You know, I tried to explain over the phone, but I think you might have been a little too... hysterical and I don't think you heard me. We do have a suspect in custody, so you're perfectly safe."

"Thank you," she said with a mock sigh. "That makes me feel a lot better."

"Her ex didn't have an alibi for that night, and everyone we interviewed seemed to think that he wanted to hurt Jen for breaking up with him. We're questioning him now."

"That's good."

"Yes. So, you see, this is all being handled and you really have nothing to fear."

"I'm glad," she said, trying to force her biggest and best smile. "You got a suspect really fast. You must be very dedicated to your job."

"Yeah," he chuckled. "My wife thinks I'm a little *too* dedicated."

"O-oh... You're married?"

"Yup. Six yeas next month. And I'm still crazy about her," he blushed.

She sighed and reached into her pocket.

"You're just like Jen," she said.

"Excuse me?"

"You can't see a good thing when it's standing right in front of you."

He had a puzzled expression on his face, but his eyes widened with realization before she even pulled out the knife.

"It was you."

THE END

Love You Always

raquel rodriguez

Jolee

I stare at the TV, my eyes sometimes flickering to Ana.

Her eyes are glued to the screen where a fighting scene is playing. Action music plays on a low volume in the background.

History books with faded covers and ripped pages clutter the clean wood floor of the living room. What Ana doesn't know is these 'history books' are filled with techniques. Special techniques.

"Do you want a glass of water?" I ask, turning my head in her direction.

Ana doesn't break eye contact with the TV, as if they're having a stare-down. She clears her throat again, and I take it as a yes.

The kitchen light is off, and all is silent except for the silent hum of the refrigerator. I grab a glass of water from one cabinet and stride over to the glowing water filters. My eyes flicker to the bottle of poison hidden with the enormous bottles of vitamins.

If I wanted to, I could. I have a chance right now. No, I'm doing this myself. She dies of 'natural' causes. A heart attack. Panic attack. Maybe not.

I resist the temptation to poison her drink. She doesn't trust me enough yet.

The sound of water dripping into the jar distracts me, and I call, "Ice or not?"

"Uh... I'll take it with ice," she says, her voice dull like a razor that's been overused.

"Alright,"

I run back to the couch, passing her the glass. She hesitates and breaks eye contact with the TV, checking the water.

A frown forms on her face, and I grin, applauding myself for making the right decision.

"Is something wrong?" I say as I watch her.

Her eyes widen at me, and she shakes her head. "Nah."

Her shoulder presses against mine and I hear her calm breaths. Neither of us says a word as she slides her arm around my shoulder like a snake. The movie continues, and I rest my head on her shoulder. I need to hurry this up.

I pull a knife out of my pocket and drive it towards her neck in a flash, my other arm tight around her neck like a python with a mouse.

Ana grunts in surprise, a gasp fleeing her crusty lips.

The needle from my pocket sinks into the back of her head and she falls to the floor, paralyzed. I lie on top of her, stroking her hair.

"I did like you," I say, resting my face on her cheek for a second. "Still though, they sent me here, not to fall in love with you."

I grab her by the arm and drag her into my closet, where she will remain until tomorrow.

My hands are blood-free, and I flop down on the couch again, wanting to sleep.

The annoying blare of my phone goes off, and I groan, standing up.

Now, I have to deal with the stupid guy outside.

Harlow

This'll be a piece of cake.

I watch her make her way toward her cell phone and grin.

Her hand touches the phone for a second, but she hesitates as she sees the caller ID. Her hands shake as it hovers in the air, wondering what to do.

She ignores the phone, biting her lip, glancing around in alarm.

They tell me she's dangerous, but she looks paranoid.

My knife calls my attention, and I put my hand over it in my pocket.

The thought of her blood splattered on the walls is a dream, but it's about to become a reality.

I creep around the house, healthy, green grass tickling my feet the entire time. My eyes stay on the girl, never lose sight of her. Her name is Jolee Harper, she's 27 and single, and she lives alone on 45 West Street.

The wind whistles in my ears as I look for an entrance, trying all the doors and windows. I come across one window that isn't locked and open it.

Jolee's house is pretty quiet, besides the whole horror movie in the back. I try to resist the urge to snicker.

She's supposed to be the strongest fighter in this whole thing. No way, she's just lucky. It can't be.

My eyes adjust to the darkness, and I recognize this as Jolee's bedroom. I make my way to the living room, knife in hand. When I enter, though, the room is empty. I sigh.

Guess this happens when you take your eyes off someone for a second.

Sharp pain shoots up my body and I let out a gasp. A hard blow to the back of my head makes me black out for a minute. I turn around to see Jolee. She stares at me with a huge grin on her face, a butterfly knife in one hand and her phone in the other.

"I don't appreciate people calling me late at night," she says, a feral snarl plastered on her face.

I roll my eyes, body shaking as I try to stand. "Put the knife down, you don't know how to use it."

Jolee's eyes narrow, and she purses her lips, raising the knife above me. "Like hell I don't!"

Jolee

"What the hell do you want, loser?" I exclaim, grabbing a knife off the dresser next to me and throwing it at him.

"You missed," Harlow says to me, sliding out of the way.

I nod, stretching my arms. "I know, did that on purpose, stupid."

"Where were you last night?"

My eyes widen, and I look up at Harlow. "Oh, I was... with my friend."

"Sure you were. You don't have any friends. Unless you're talking about dead people," - he glared at me, his arms crossed - "then they don't count. So who were you REALLY with?"

"You know the answer, stupid. I was at the club." I inhale the cigarette smoke and burst out coughing, waving the surrounding air. "Gosh, didn't I tell you to stop smoking?"

I grab the knife off the table next to me and aim it at his cigarette. Then I pull my hand back and throw it.

Harlow's eyes widen and he jumps back, but the cigarette is nailed to the wall.

"Shit, Jolee!" he exclaims, shaking his hand.

He storms toward me, his hand is the air. I don't flinch at all, just stare at him as he stands above me.

His hand impacts my face and pushes my head to the side.

"I'm leaving." Standing up from the couch, I shove him away, running out the door.

Harlow watches me, rolling his eyes. "Fine with me," he says, sitting down where I was sitting down before.

"Gosh, I wish I'd killed you when I got the chance," I mutter, my hands in my pockets.

"Right back at you," he calls, and I slam the door behind me.

THE END

Spectrum

Lauren Chan

I was arrested in a country bar. At eleven o'clock, while I was sipping Gin and Tonic in the morning.

I saw the police cruisers pull into the gravel lot. The sound of their footsteps on the mud getting stronger. They were moving fast and crunched to a stop. Outside, the rain had stopped, but the entrance door was still pebbled with bright drops. Dark sullen clouds were rolling about in the sky. Thunder and lightning here and there. Lightbars flashing and popping. Red and blue light in the raindrops on the glass door of the bar. Doors burst open, and the policemen jumped out. Two from each car, weapons ready. One revolver, one rifle, two shotguns. One rifle and one shotgun ran to the back.

I just sat and watched them. This operation was for me. Not for any other in the bar. These people had been in this city for their whole lives. I had been in this city for only two hours, fifty-minutes, thirty-one seconds, and counting.

Silence was swirling in the bar, a dirty cloud of smoke, the stagnant stench of cigarettes hidden within the collaboration of mephitic odors. There was even a hint of the sick, musty smell of alcohol and sweat tainting the air.

This was heavy stuff. The guy with the revolver stayed at the door. They were fit and lean. Neat. Textbook moves. The other shotgun was doing a good job of staying at the door, he could splatter me with a degree of accuracy. So far they had the advantage. They were doing right.

"Freeze! Police!" Revolver yelled.

He was blowing off his tension and trying to scare me. Again, textbook moves. Predictable. Plenty of sound and fury to soften the target. Scare, maybe? I raised my hands. The guy with the shotgun started in from the door. The guy with the revolver came closer. Too close. Their first error. If I had to, I might have lunged for the revolver and forced it up. A blast into the ceiling, an elbow into the policeman's face, and the gun could have been mine. The guy with the shotgun had narrowed his angle and couldn't risk hitting his partner. It could have ended badly for them. But I just sat there, hands raised on the bar stool.

I slid slowly out of the stool and extended my wrists to the officer with the revolver. I would not say anything for now. Not if they brought along their whole police department with howitzers.

The revolver was the sergeant. The shotgun and rifle covered me as the sergeant holstered his revolver and unclipped the handcuffs from his belt, and clicked them on my wrists. The backup team came in through the back and took up position behind me. Very thorough.

The shotgun still covered me. The sergeant stepped up in front. He was an athletic man. Bulky and tanned. My age. The acetate nameplate above his shirt pocket said: Romano. He looked up at me.

"You are under arrest for murder," he said. "You have the right to remain silent. Anything you say may be used as evidence against you. You have the right to representation by an attorney. Should you be unable to afford an attorney, one will be appointed for you by the State of Texas free of charge. Do you understand these rights?"

He spoke clearly. He didn't read it from a card. He spoke like he knew what it meant and why it was important. To him and me. I didn't respond.

"Do you understand your rights?" he said again.

Again I didn't respond. Long experience had taught me that absolute silence is the best way. Say something, and it can be misheard. Misunderstood. Misinterpreted. It can get you

145

convicted. It can get you killed. Silence upsets the arresting officer. He has to tell you silence is your right but he hates it if you exercise that right. I was being arrested for murder. But I said nothing.

"Do you understand your rights?" the guy called Romano asked me again. "Do you even speak English?"

He was calm. I said nothing. He remained calm. He had the calm of a man whose moment of danger had passed. He would just drive me to the station house and then I would become someone else's problem. He glanced around his three fellow officers.

"OK, make a note, he's said nothing," he grunted. "Let's go."

* * *

Romano still stared at me as the car slowed to yaw into the approach to the station house. The words: Texas Police Headquarters, embossed in teakwood on a huge white building. I thought: should I be worried? I was under arrest. In a town where I'd never been before. Apparently for murder. But I knew two things. First, they couldn't prove something had happened if it hadn't happened. And second, I hadn't killed anybody.

Not in their town, and not for a long time, anyway.

* * *

They put me in a cell with dull grey walls and one-way glass. The cell only had two chairs and a table, opposite to which a woman was pushing me into making a statement, a confession for a crime I did not commit. Silence was the only thing that greeted the cassette recorder.

Seconds turned into minutes. Time was passing by quickly.

I stared at the women. She was new to this. This was probably the first or the second time she was doing this. A university graduate, maybe? She spoke as if she was vomiting out whatever she had learned in her college. I was an average student in school. It barely taught me anything.

After forty minutes of pure silence, the cell door opened to reveal two men. Both were built and strong. If it weren't for their uniforms, I'd mistake them for dealers, the shady ones. They had the 'no-nonsense-look' on, probably annoyed at my silence. Intimidation would probably work on others here. But not me. The woman with the cassette went out of the room. Sad. I liked her.

"My name is Jameson.", the first guy said, or rather, yelled. "I am the chief of this department's detective bureau. Now, listen up, I will not be taking anymore of this silent treatment. You better start talking or rot here in jail.", he sneered. Acknowledging the shake of the head of the other guy, he walked away.

"I am Steve. Rank's captain.", the second guy started. "Before we go on, you have not confirmed your rights. Do you understand them?"

I answered affirmatively. He nodded.

"You have been charged with murder. You will need a lawyer. Do you want the state to provide you one, free of charge?"

"No." I kept my responses short.

Steve handed me a form and gestured to go through it and put my signature. It was a release.

"You've been advised you may have a lawyer, and we'll provide one, free of charge, but you don't want one."

I nodded.

"We will start with your name, address, and occupation.", he said.

I remained silent.

He sighed, "You carry no ID, no license, no cash or card. No identity. Who are you?"

I stared at the glass window, catching a reflection of myself, knowing for a fact that Romano and the other guys were watching this.

"Why am I here?" I asked.

"You know why you are here. Call it homicide for now. Since you deny the claim to have murdered. The scene was disturbing. His organs had been ripped out. His eyes were gouged and his tongue was cut. Tell me, what do the initials W.S.C mean to you?"

I raised an eyebrow.

"It was carved on his arm, the victim. The witness reported a white guy, wearing an overcoat, dark hair, no luggage, and looked as if he was around his mid-thirties, walking down there, just after he noticed the body. Gave him quite a fright."

I was a white guy, wearing an overcoat, had dark hair, carried no baggage, and was around my mid-thirties. I reached this city at eight in the morning. Walking through the main road. I was in the bar at eleven. And right now it was half-past two.

"How far is the main road from here?" I asked.

"About three hours."

"So, you are saying that exactly after killing this guy, I teleported to a bar and sat there, waiting for the police to find out? I started from the main road at eight, reached the bar at eleven. It took me three hours then and there itself if the highway is three hours away. Plenty of people must have seen me while I was walking down."

Steve stared at his hands for a long time. He didn't respond.

The guy was doing his job, but he was wasting my time.

"OK, Steve," I said. "I'll make a statement describing every little thing I did since I entered your lousy town limits until I got hauled in here in the middle of my drink. If you can make anything out of it, I'll give you a damn medal. Because all I did was to place one foot in front of the other for nearly three hours in the pouring rain all the way through your precious highway."

I breathed heavily. I lost control of my temper for a moment.

"Don't get smart with me. You're in deep stuff. Bad things happened up there. Our witness saw you leaving the scene. You're a stranger with no ID and no story.", he said, tapping his fingers against the table.

"I wasn't leaving a homicide scene," I said. "I was walking down the road. There's a difference, alright? People leaving homicide scenes run and hide. They don't walk straight down the road. What's wrong with walking down a road? People walk down roads all the time, don't they?"

"You were a detective yourself, weren't you?"

I stiffened visibly. I *was* a detective and worked with the military.

"My name is Zach. Zach Amrose."

His eyes narrowed. "I-"

The cell door opened once again, and Romano came bursting in.

"He is lying. Put him on the sixth level. *Not* a holding cell. The chief thought he had seen you before, now he remembered where.", he yelled.

He looked at me in the eyes and said, "Amrose is dead. He has been for a long time."

He then looked at Steve and said, "His prints match that of the killer. We ran the diagnostics thrice."

I was surprised.

There was no point in trying to justify myself. I wasn't lying. Lying got you nowhere.

But the truth got me put in a cell. I looked at Steve and told him, "How did they get my prints when I carried nothing?"

Steve stared at me for a long time.

I continued, "20B. That's the bus number. I was there at eight. Even if Jameson says he saw me, how could he when this is the first time I have stepped foot into this town? Ask the locals. Heck, ask the bar. Plus, wasn't Jameson at the crime scene during that time?"

Steve's eyes widened for a brief moment. "You could be lying."

I gave him a blank look, "Why would I?"

"What does it mean? *W.S.C*? " he asked.

"West Side Cartel."

Detective Steve ran out of the sixth level as soon as he heard the name. The most ruthless crime family. And Jameson was part of it. And if he had his hands on the city database, this was just the beginning of chaos.

THE END

Braden Bates: Mystery of The Clay Tablet

Alice Raymond

"It's her." Braden said coldly. His auburn hair flew all around him in the strong autumn wind and his wire-rimmed glasses didn't even come close to mitigating the cold, ruthless, calculating look of detective who has caught his criminal in his hazel eyes.

"Braden, it's not that I don't trust you, but I don't think May could **possibly** be the criminal here." Dominick said, gazing uncertainly at the girl roughly 10 meters ahead of us. She was his little sister, May, who was apparently our prime suspect in the recent robbery of Sargon The Great's clay tablet. We were part-time detectives; all four of us had other jobs that we were completely invested in. Only Braden was a part-time social media manger; he spent the better part of his time searching the deep web for cases of thefts, murder, scandals and practically any other criminal case you could think of. The rest of us were basically just sidekicks.

May and Dominick actually looked very much alike, both sharing the same dirty blonde hair, hazel-grey eyes and rosy cheeks. The only differences between them were the ages and height. Where

Dominick was the tallest of my friends, over 6 feet, May was a short little petite girl, barely grazing the 5'4 mark.

"It all adds up." Braden said, feeling for his pistol in the pocket of his red trench coat.

"You don't say." Ari mused, running a hand through her waist-length straight raven hair.

"There's only one person it could be. May Coulomb has been associating with people known for atrocious robberies as of late and been headed to all the wrong places. All after Sargon the Great's clay tablet went missing from the Museum of Asian History." Braden said.

"But May..." Dominick began, looking wistfully at the girl we knew as his younger sister.

"Hate to say it, Brady, but he right here, brother. And sorry for the pun, but May Coulomb is just not the kind of person who would steal such a valuable artifact. Why, she's a child! I doubt she even knew the thing existed before the news made international headlines." Ari exclaimed.

"Ari's right. Braden, we honestly don't doubt your "superior sleuthing skills", but is May Coulomb really the perp we're looking for?" I questioned him with the vague feeling that the three of us were trying to break Braden down in a way similar to how you and your teammates would break down the Boss in a videogame. A wave of triumph passed through me at the briefest of flickers in his hazel orbs.

"She is, Emma." Braden hissed, the coldness returning to his eyes, all the emotion drained from his voice and face. Tears pooled in my eyes. May was like a little sister to us all; how on Earth could Braden treat her like a criminal?

"A good detective doesn't let his or her personal affiliations get in the way of work, Em. If we didn't know May personally, she'd already be before the jury for trial." Braden suddenly said without looking at me, as if he was reading my thoughts.

"The call's on you." Ari said, looking pointedly at me. I gulped, the cold autumn air foreign against my esophagus.

"We're waiting for you." Braden said, glaring at me accusingly. I looked away if only to not face the hostility in his eyes.

"May's fate is in your hands, Emma." Dominick whispered, looking away.

I hated being put on the spot like this.

"I'm sorry, Dominick. If May is really the criminal here, however unlikely it seems, we have to put aside our love for her and bring justice." I breathed.

155

"Then pounce." Ari mumbled. And from the look behind her eyes, I could tell she was brazing herself for the inevitable.

"May Coulomb, you are under arrest for the theft of the original Clay Tablet inscribed with Sargon The Great's will." Braden announced, with the 9mm semi-automatic handgun at the back of her head. "Do not resist. Move an inch and I'll shoot."

"Braden?!" May called, coming face to face with Braden's infamous look of victory.

"Do. Not. Resist." Braden hissed with the likeness of a snake.

"Me?! Braden, you know me! Do you honestly think *I'm* the one behind this?!" she demanded.

"Yes."

"Braden, no! You're wrong! I-I'm just a kid! I'm 17!" she wailed. I wished the Earth would swallow me whole. I'd rather be faced with the electric chair than this torture.

"A kid, huh? Maybe you should have thougt of that **before** you stole a priceless relic, criminal."

"Criminal? Braden h-ho-how-how can you?" the poor thing cried.

"I know May Coulomb, not the criminal who stole the Clay Tablet."

"I'm still May Coulomb, no! Don't, Braden!"

"May Coulomb... is... dead."

156

"You **know** me! Emma, do you believe him? Ari? You're here too?! And-" That's about when May's eyes fell on Dominick.

All the fight drained from her face, leaving us with a hollow shell of the girl we knew. Putting on a mask of stoicism, May said "My own brother thinks I did it? Then it doesn't even matter. Handcuff me, put me through a farce of a trial, throw me into a cell with rats or hang me. I don't care anymore."

"May..." Ari began, a flicker of uncertainty in her copper-sulphate blue eyes.

"May the Devil be with me." May hissed. "Jesus Christ doesn't care for me no more."

"Good. Maybe they'll let you off the hook with 20 years if you plead guilty." Braden jeered. I didn't have to look over my shoulder to know the look of utter misery on Dominick's face.

It was the shove that made Braden go 'nuclear', as I called it. May pushed him off her with the force of a rabbit, and it triggered our bipolar man. Braden kicked poor May onto the cobblestone with 50 times the force she'd shoved him with. The dull thud of her back on the stone made bile rise at the back of my throat.

"You dare-" Braden began, but high-pitched maniacal laughter made all of our eyes turn the other way.

157

A man was running in the opposite direction, with a black duffel bag in hand. A small piece of something stuck at the end of the zipper. And we didn't need any confirmation – May *wasn't* the thief at all. Maniacal Laugh was our man.

The tell-tale tip of clay-yellow from was a dead giveaway.

THE END

Insane

Black Raven

"...there's nothing you can do," Was the last thing she said before plunging a knife inside me. And that's where she was wrong.

It all had started with a break-in in Clark's bakery. The only thing stolen? A top-secret ingredient they refused to talk about. As you can imagine, you can't really find anything without knowing what it is or at least what it looks like. We tried questioning the staff, yet the only thing we got out was that the ingredient was stored in a little black box in the shop's safe. Nothing about what it actually was or why they were so desperate to find it. Since they said it was "confidential." Confidential my *ss! At this point, I was hellbent on getting out of this case. Like what the hell?! They wanted us to find it like it was the end of the f*cking world and at the same time wouldn't tell us sh*t about anything. I was sure that any case was more important than this.

Well, that is, 'till I saw the owner's daughter. Ruby Clark. She was as beautiful as day, yet that wasn't what kept me. Though, her relationship with her father was. They both knew something. Something big. And they disagreed on what to do with it. So I did some research. I couldn't find anything about their daughter, deciding to focus on the bakery.

The shop had gone bankrupt a year ago. Yet, it had magically paid up its debts a month ago, when newfound customers started surging in. Buying everything as if they were addicted. 'How good was this ingredient that it made people buy so much of it?' I thought as I grew even more suspicious.

"Kai, come here," Jane said.

"What is it? I'm working here." I said, kinda annoyed. She would always call me for stupid things like today is someone's birthday and sh*t.

"Wow! Is that any way to treat your best friend who may have just found a breakthrough for the case?" She pouted. Oh, I forgot. She also works in evidence, so she can be pretty useful.

"Great! Tell me." Maybe she found something about what the ingredient is.

"Why should I after you treated me in such way?" She said. Right hand pressed against her forehead and rapidly flapping eyelashes.

"We are not doing this again," I said sternly.

"Then I won't tell you anything!" She said, mad that I didn't give in. Ugh. What a pain! I knew she was the only good for anything

160

person in the department, but god, I hated when she got like that.

"Okay, I give in. I'll buy you lunch tomorrow," I said, begrudgingly.

"Thanks!" She smiled excitedly. "So, you know how the cameras at the bakery were broken, and we couldn't find any data?"

"Yes," I urged her to keep on.

"Well, the store in front had one, and you can clearly see how Ruby Clark was the last one to enter the store. Now we just have to show this to the others and interrogate her." She said, leaving.

"Wait! No!" I yelled, reaching up to her and grabbing her arm. I can't let anyone else find about this. Not yet, anyway.

"What's wrong?" She asked, shock adorning her features.

"What if you let me handle it? Alone I mean." At first, she looked confused, but then her expression changed to realization and finally landed on mischief. Uh oh. What could she be planning now?

"Oooh. Does someone have a crush on little old Ruby and wants to save her." She wiggled her eyebrows.

"What?! No! I have barely met the woman! Get your mind of the gutter!" I shouted.

161

"You are such a killjoy!" She sulked. "Anyway, you know the price. Cya."

"N-" I tried to refuse, but she had already left. Oh god! This woman! She really plans to charge me for keeping this a secret. I'm gonna have to ask for a raise if I want to keep doing this.

Sometime later at Ruby's house:

"Can you explain this?" I showed Ruby the security video.

"That doesn't say anything. I could have just been looking for something I left there." She argued, feigning ignorance.

"Funny how you say that, when you rarely go there and even more when you were the last one to leave," I pointed out. There was something up in this family, and I was going to find out.

"That still doesn't say anything. Someone could have just opened it with the key before I got there." She barked. 'Though nut to crack, huh? Let's see what she'll do with this!' I thought.

"Interesting, you mentioning a key. If I remember right, only your father and a few staff knew that the padlock didn't work and that you had to use a key. So, how do YOU know?" I inquired.

Her face froze. Body stiffened.

"Well, what is the answer? I'm waiting." This was the last blow. There was no way she could answer that without digging herself even deeper!

162

"I'm going to give you two options. One, tell me what's REALLY going on here, or two, get arrested for burglary." There was no way she wouldn't give in now! At least, that's what I believed.

"Then, I may as well get arrested." Her voice filled with confidence. The mask was perfect. Except it had a crack. Her eyes. They were filled with fear. She didn't want to go to prison. I knew that. What I didn't know was why.

"I know there's something wrong. I can help you. You just have to let me." I pleaded.

She looked into my eyes. Analyzing my soul. A sigh escaped her lips.

"The secret component is a drug." She said, tired.

"What?! A drug?! Are you sure about this?" I couldn't stop thinking about it. It was crazy!

"Yes, it's a new drug, my dad's chemists made. It hasn't been tested thoroughly, so it's being experimented on the customers." She tiredly lays back on the sofa. The light, making the eyebags on her eyes visible.

"You didn't know, did you?" I sat next to her.

"No, I didn't. I found out the other day when dad called and said he wanted me to continue the 'family business.'" The sadness in her expression visible to the world. "I was shocked. Like what was

I supposed to do, you know? I tried to convince him to stop...he wouldn't budge."

"Why didn't you go to the police?"

"Hahaha...Hahaha...Hahaha..." She was laughing her head off 'till, "Wait. Are you serious? You are, aren't you?" She looked at me as if I were crazy. "How could I go to the police? He's my father, man."

"You are telling me. I'm a detective."

"'Cause I realized that there was only one way to stop my father...death." She made her hands into a fist.

"Death?! You're gonna kill him?" She was insane.

"Don't get me wrong here, I didn't want to kill him," I relaxed. "but that's what I had to do." She gets up and takes a knife from the drawer.

How could I have missed it? She isn't going to kill him. She already killed him.

"The feeling that I got was ecstatic. I need more. Correction. I'm gonna get more! And there's nothing you can do." She added, stabbing me with the knife. At this moment, I hated my decision to skip my self-defense classes.

"There's gotta be something I missed here. Didn't you love your father?" I asked, trying to dodge the other hits.

"I did...or...maybe I didn't. That doesn't matter now, though. The only thing I want is blood! To see it flowing out of your body! It gives me such a thrill!" Her smile, widening every step she took closer. "I didn't want to kill you. I tried to contain it all. But you kept questioning so, I decided to play innocent for a while and then... 'twat'"

The knife hit me once again. I knew I couldn't take another hit. The pain was unbearable, but I would soon escape it.

Did she kill me? Well, no! 'Cause as it's clearly seen, I'm still telling the story. What happened was that contrary to what you and she believed, I wasn't here alone. Jane, though a good friend, wasn't one to keep secrets so, as you can guess, the whole police station was spying on me and knew where I was. Reinforcement got there in a second and saved me from that psychopath.

In the end, they found out that Ruby was bipolar. She had stopped taking her medicine somedays before he stole the drug. Fooled me well. I could have sworn she was a sane person. Guess you never really know these things.

THE END

Through Dilemmas and Beers

Andrew Parker

Do you mind if I sit here?

Do you know the trolley problem? It supposes to be a philosophy and ethic series of theoretical question to say how much you would sacrifice to preserve something. I am not a philosopher, but I think about this every day. Why? Because I'm living inside a trolley problem.

Please, don't leave. Sit here, and I will tell you my story. A great story, I promise you will like it. Come on. I will pay you a round of beer. The beer here worth every penny. I won't keep you long. Come on. Thanks for keeping me company. Berny, my man, bring two from the top shelf.

Let's see, when is the best moment to start my story? The beginning? Every moment is the beginning of something and the end of many more—Right, no philosophy bullshit, only the facts.

I was a cop, a negotiator before I become a private. You are too young to know, but in the late '80s, some people moved to a big farm on the county's edgy. New age folks, searching for their own utopia. Although this is a free country and people are free to believe in wherever they wanted, we put a couple of eyes on these outsiders. Something didn't seem right in there.

Thanks, Berny. One for me and one for you, Nick. Cheers.

I only enter the scene in 99, when some letters were delivered to the local news and the mayor, declaring the end of the world and war against capitalism. I was called to decipher and deal with the terrorist. At that time, we didn't use the word terrorists. The "nine-eleven" put this term in everybody months. Anyway, I did my job, did an investigation, and discover the culprits, the reasons, and the plans. As you can deduce, the Solar Ethereal Temple, as they called themselves, were the men behind the letters. They had some rotten apples brainwashing people to believe that killing people was the best way to win friends and to influence others. Lunatics. Skipping the details of the cop work. I discover they were planning to detonate some buildings, and we lack the proof to make the politician move their butts and take the threat seriously. Lives were in danger, and they needed a full filled form before looking us in the eyes. Dammit.

Sorry, until today, this bothers me. Give me a minute to cool down my nerves. The beer is good, isn't it?

Long story short, the probable targets were three residential buildings, all homes to the new rich, the ones who made a fortune in the early internet. The cult believed that by killing the owners of those businesses, they would get more attention for the cause. As I said, there were lunatics. My problem was the lack of people and time. There weren't enough people to cover all the places nor time to evacuate everybody properly before everything exploded. I had people barking in my ears and tough choices to make. News, politicians, NGOs, lawyers, the whole circus had a concern about the situation.

I made my choice, and I accept the consequences. I tried to consider the situation as a whole, measuring everything, but I made mistakes, terrible mistakes. All the targets had explosives. I saved a hundred and eleven lives, but I lost fifty-four. This isn't a math problem to have a balance. Human lives. Their stories were abruptly ended because of my decisions. The internal affairs said I did the best with the resources, and we have enough proofs to put the cult's leader behind bars. The case was considered a minor success, but I know deep down I made a mistake.

Did you have already finished? Berny, two more, please.

Days later, I found the way I should have acted to save everybody, but time isn't a boomerang, right? If I had left my team and handle myself the third one, I might have saved those fifty-four lives, a full deck of cards. I had some courses on explosives. A person can't be over-prepared. I had the skills to solve, although not the practice needed. That attempt would have better odds of a complete success than what actually happened. Things couldn't end up worse. Of course, I could die, but be a victim of your own mistakes is better than just watch the mess you made. Do you understand me?

Wednesday is the calmest day here. Only people with problems come to a bar on a Wednesday. Another round.

I went to all the funerals I could, showing my face to be insulted by those who survive and the decease's families. I needed to do that. Are you a believer? Sorry, no philosophy, just curiosity. I was raised in a catholic house, and as one, asking for forgiveness and making amends is part of my core, even after I start to question the bible. The funerals weren't enough for me. I need to do more for them.

I ask for some favors and spend some late nights searching to make a profile for everyone that died in the incident. I had a complete profile with personal life, job, family, even some secrets, skeletons in the closet. I was measuring the damage I have made. It was one of the dumbest ideas I have ever had. Soon, the situation wasn't theoretical anymore. It became practical, and at that moment, I know in detail what I have done. Each aspect I didn't notice and all the consequences. The worst, I didn't have any idea what to do next. I create something without purpose, except to torment myself.

169

I keep my position until the end of the trials, and the lunatics were sent to jail. They tried to plead, but at this moment, I had already asked for retirement. I had something to live on and a tiny share of the cider's family business to help with the bills. I still had energy, and my mind was as sharp as ever, so I decided to devote my life to make amends to those who have died.

All this was just the introductions. Berny, please, bring another round, a jar of water, and peanuts too. My grandma always said to me to prevent a hangover by drinking water.

I become private, and my first goal was to make sure everybody receives what they deserve from the insurance company. The first thing I learn was money attracted problems as honey attracts bears. Don't you agree? I had to show what I had gathered to allow some people apart from the official family to receive some help. Oh boy, I made some dangerous enemies, deceived wives, and traditionalist's parents are terrible. I receive some cruel mail, and I lost a great car within two years.

My next goal was to preserve the legacy. These people had jobs, dreams, projects, many already in process. I didn't want that to all get lost because they had died in a stupid mistake, my mistake. I tried to make sure to stop any crook attempt to steal the business they had build through nights without sleep in their parent's garage. White-collar criminals think they are smart and less dangerous than other thugs, but they are as vicious as any other bandit. Believe it or not, I enter in some gunfights and exchange some punches to complete this task. Some families got really mad with the mess I made and the dirt I discovered. I had to exchange houses to escape from the rocks and eggs thrown at my window in the middle of the night.

The legacy plan wasn't over yet. Almost two years and a half later, and with some gray hair saying hello, I enter the hobbies parts. As soon rich people become really rich, they seem to discover that to gain a rich badge, they need to support some NGO or found one. NGO's can be a real snake's nest and hide all sorts of creepy things. Money laundering, pedophile rings, drugs, human exploitation, and more. Please don't misinterpret me. The legit business also exists. They do important work with quality and honesty. I have a theory: The problem with paradises is that eventually, a snake will appear and make everybody be exiled. I don't know my role in this allegory: snake, apple, or the angry god.

My adventure in this world cost me some days in the hospital, strange memories, and more dead people in my account, new cards for my deck. My girlfriend called me crazy, stop accept my calls, leaving my life for good. People started to look strange at me. A good friend, my best friend, said I was punishing myself and creating a shit storm whatever I go. He is right, but I have much to do to compensate for what I have done. I wasn't over yet.

Do you want to eat something? They have hot wings here, delicious ones. Excellent, Berny, bring hot wings, and the lasts bottles for both of us.

These jobs were pro bono, using the term the lawyers love. Don't you love it? I have other cases. The typical ones are missing people, cheating ones, and paranoics. Those were the cases that paid my bills but didn't clean my souls. The NGOs took me more than three years to solve- well, there are still some loose ends I am working on, but the majority is over, and I am only dealing with the consequences now. When I think I find the end of a line, it launches me into a rabbit hole. My life is a rollercoaster.

Did you get the trolley part? The trolley problem haunts me. For example, I discovered that the money that helps people living in the streets of this city comes from a crime lord. If I blew the whistle on that situation, everything would vanish the moment I hang up the phone. Yes, I was an accomplice in a crime. Not my first, not my last. Other situations like that had happened: a person supports free clinics killed several hookers, companies which offer job opportunities also sell illegal immigrant as slaves, a whole building was being exploited by a diplomat's son, one whose the parents are great people and didn't have a clue about his son's behavior. I was seeing more crimes without the badger than with one. Before your eyes pop the sockets, I didn't make the three monkeys for all crimes. I had denounced the majority, winning tons of hate as a reward for the good deed. Of course, new cards came to my hand too, some I thought had prevented.

Great! Here's the food, you need to try this sauce is to die for. Don't need to hurry, enjoy the meal, and have your time. In last than an hour, you will be wherever you want to be, far from me. If you are on the clock, I call you a uber when we end the wings. I promise you.

Where did I stop? Right, the hard choices. I extend my debt to compensate the deceased's love one too. I deliver my card at the funerals, and months, years later, some come asking for help. I accept these cases, most simple like the cases which paid my bills. Others were bigger than I could bite. One father saves every penny to put the only daughter in a good university but dies. The heirs spent all as the world was on fire, and when the well dry, they came with crocodile's tears looking for me. I have a code of honor, but I am not stupid - or maybe I am. I sold my car to help her. I sold many things to help cases like that. Cars, small properties, my part in the cider company, and a part of my savings all invest in keeping some dreams still alive. By the way, no thanks or hugs as payment, just insults, mean gazes, and in the best-case scenario, nothing. Now, my belongings maybe fit in a travel bag.

Do you know the pain of being shot? No, great, I hope you never discover. In my line of work, gun wounds and broken bones are expected if you are doing a good job. And if this is a trustful measure for good work, I may be pretty good. Eight shots, four broken ribs, one arm, and some burns. Scars all over the body. Each one taught me a valorous lesson about lockpick, talk with each urban tribe, get the best from cars, run, act, drunk, and others. Many lessons I learned, many injuries I accepted to fulfill my goals. I had to found another insurance firm because the old said I was a liability. Sorry, I daydream a little.

Berny, my man, the bill. Where is the uber going to? Maple Ville. Fifteen minutes. The traffic on the east side is terrible. Don't be silly, it is freezing outside, wait in here. Maple Ville- I know the place, nice one. Finish your drink.

Over with the small talk. I have to say that you are a strange man, Nick. I came to you knowing your name without ever meet each other, and it took you almost twenty minutes to notice the strangeness. Don't even think about running. You are so drunk that you can't even crawl. Calm down. I don't want to hurt you or make a fuzz. What do I want? I thought my story made it clear. You need to pay more attention, Nick. I want to make peace with

174

my deads, and you have the opportunity to make me a solid. Nick, please, don't make me show how not drunk I am and how fast I make you a new pee hole.

Nice, good to know you still have something between the ears. I have a profile with your name on it, a thick one. Family, work, friends, lovers, hobbies, passions, name something it will be in there. I did my homework. I want to be clear, I am blackmailing you. You will be selected to represent a big shot in the cult case, sentence review, maybe you already know this, and this is your reason to be here. Anyway, you are an excellent lawyer and is quite sure you can free the man from jail. I don't want it, you don't want it too, because if you take the case, I will put your old client's secrets on the news. By the way, you should change your locks and keys. You know how your old clients deal with leak information. Right, you would meet the farm. Just to you know how deeply concern I am with your health, I know what is in Havana street, 222, and I have copies of this archive in a safe place.

I don't want that anything harmful happens to you. On the contrary, I want you well, taking good care of your life and loved ones. In fact, I believe you should take a vacation to somewhere warm. Tonight, when you enter your cozy home, call your office saying you deserve a month off. Please take this ticket to Mexico.

It cost me my last miles, so accept as a gift. Everybody will be happy if you decline this case and take a tan on the beach, right?

The driver is two minutes from here, better move. I will accompany you. See? I told you that you are drunk as a skunk. Lean on me, right. Almost there. Hang in there just a bit. The cold will help you get better and think clearly. Keep breathing. The car is almost here. As I said, this is your car, Nicolas Johnson Smith. Have a good trip, and don't forget to pack your baggage.

Berny, my boy, how much I owe you for your help tonight?

THE END

176

A Memory that Counts

Parker Barlow

The Crowe family farmhouse stood two stories high in a flat field of windswept broom grass. Ivy climbed the barbed wire fences that designated pastures for the six head o' cattle that lowed, often, in the lower field—the one down by the creek and the parallel rows of pulp pine. A huge, largely unused barn opposed the house roughly two acres away. A single silo leaned slightly to the left—too tired to stand upright, too proud to downright lie. The farmhouse, especially after the trauma from recent events, protruded like an exposed beating heart, and the farm, overall, replaced emptiness with an abundance of absence.

"One hundred seventy-eight, one hundred seventy-nine, one eighty. My-ma memoried."

Inside the farmhouse, young William sat in the shadow of a grandfather clock that stood next to an electric wall sconce at the edge of the sitting room next to the kitchen entrance. Without any consistent interval and without any discernable relation to the time itself, Will repeatedly counted off three numbers in consanguinity with the guttural tocks of the deep, elder clock:

"One hundred seventy-eight, one hundred seventy-nine, one eighty. Me-me Mauri."

Then, silence echoed across the hardwood heart-of-pine, measuring off by the clock's timing tocks, thoughts that gathered somberly as far from formidable concepts as the East was from the West.

Nancy set the money on the table between the sofa and Mr. Crowe's favorite chair, sliding it back to a neutral position between her clutches and Mr. Crowe, the man who'd just handed it to her. She hadn't counted the money, but she could tell it was a lot, more than she would make in a week of babysitting other people's children. That thought made her push the rolled wad even further in hopes that it we be morally strong enough to forget about her.

"You really don't have to pay me, Mr. Crowe."

Mr. Crowe really hadn't thought about how much Nancy had grown up. How old was she now? Sixteen? Seventeen? "Oh, I...I didn't mean to insult you, Nancy. Y'all grow up so fast."

"One hundred seventy-eight, one hundred seventy-nine, one eighty. Mento Marie."

"No. No sir. I'm not insulted. I mean, that's a lot of money."

178

"For a normal night, sure, but we have no idea when we'll be home or when...." Mr. Crowe found himself unable to finish his thought.

"Yes, sir. I know," Nancy said, noticing that the money hadn't moved. "I just want to help out, especially...."

Similarly, Nancy found herself unable to speak when her words delivered her to the memory that the Crowe's young nephew Geoffrey had recently died—drowned down by the creek while playing with Will. And with Geoffrey's invisible friend, whom the boys had at various times referred to either as Mauri or Marie. No one was really sure of any details other than the fact that one child was dead and the other would never recover, and those were the only details that counted.

"...especially...," she tried again.

Nancy was of no blood relation to the Crowes, and she lived roughly a mile away down the patched-up two-lane road. The people of Lancaster may have been dispersed widely, but their bonds were cinched tighter. The loss of a ten-year-old child was everyone's loss. And Will was everyone's fault.

Mrs. Crowe appeared in the doorway, holding her swollen belly like a fragile package.

The package inspired Nancy: "...especially since you will be home right after your little miracle is delivered unto the world."

"Yes," Mrs. Crowe agreed, smiling despite being short of breath. "Yes, our little miracle will—"

The clock struck six and played its six o'clock chimes, which would hot have, themselves, stopped Mrs. Crowe from talking about the imminent miracle, but her Will shouted his strangely familiar chant over the chimes.

"One hundred seventy-eight, one hundred seventy-nine, one eighty. Mento memory."

"She will definitely be here very soon," Mrs. Crowe said, feeling her miracle kick.

"I know where everything is," Nancy said, avoiding any extra questions before the Crowes walked out to and left in the car that had been sitting packed and ready going on a solid week now.

Nancy turned to your Will, who maintained his spot. She'd been his sitter since he was born, it seemed, (He started counting again.) but not since the incident. She stood still by the window where she'd watched Will's parents leave. The room had seemed crowded earlier, but something about the emptiness made the room seem smaller, somehow. And Will seem closer. He'd seemed, at first, to act as if he were unaware of his parents' departure, and of his own aloneness with Nancy.

"Are you hungry? You dad said you haven't eaten."

Will looked up as if to count. Instead, he stared through a tuft of hair at his standing sitter: "He knows you're here."

Nancy had to remind herself that the boy had been through a lot, especially for his age. Like Geoffrey, Will was only ten years old. Nancy had been a dependable sitter for both of the Crowe families, even keeping both for the majority of a summer while the boys' fathers worked in the fields. Farm mothers, like their husbands, worked from sun to sun, but neither worked in the house all day. And keeping the boys rescued Nancy from her own house. All the farm families were tight; some were too tight.

"Who, Will? Who knows I'm here?"

"Mo-Ree."

Nancy had heard the name before. She'd never understood it—still didn't—but Geoffrey's invisible friend became a turning point in his life. Not nearly as happy as he had been, his parents believed he'd invented the friend to replace Nancy after both boys had recently grown too old to need a sitter, as such. Geoffrey had even stopped playing with Will, or Will had stopped playing with him. No one was certain.

181

"Maybe that boy actually started believing the imaginary friend was real," Nancy's father had said about Will. "Maybe that's why he killed the other kid. Just plain old, good old jealousy. That's it. That's all it takes."

He offered Nancy a .38 snub nose revolver to take with her "just in case the little murdering psycho" struck again. She refused. He laughed, thinking Nancy was afraid of the little pistol. Nancy noticed that he put the gun back in his top drawer, and she noticed that it was loaded. She wanted to be ashamed of noticing. She wondered what her mom would think about the gun or about anything for that matter.

"Mauri?" Nancy asked. "Geoffrey's invisible friend?"

"Friend," Will repeated. "He's my friend now. And he wants to be friends with you."

Nancy thought about what her father had said. *Jealousy?* She said, "People can have more than one friend, you know."

Will did not answer, but he seemed to be enraptured by the possibility of multiple friends. Or highly disturbed.

"You know that don't you, Will?"

"One hundred seventy-eight, one hundred seventy-nine, one eighty. May man-to Mauri."

"Why do you do that? Why do you count like that?"

"Mo-ree!"

"That's not a real...." Nancy remembered that Will's parents had called her to protect, not to upset, the child.

That money that sat on the table, she decided, would stay there. She was scared—chilled—but there was no one she could call even if she'd have wanted to. Will's parents were busy with their miracle, her own father was the worst monster she knew, and her friends' parents wouldn't allow them to help her babysit a known killer.

"I didn't kill...," Will began. "I didn't kill those chickens in the barn. And I didn't steal the food we had out for Sunday."

His tears drew her in.

"I didn't hear about that," she said.

"Mom said.... Mom and Dad said it showed that I still had the streak."

"The streak?"

He didn't answer.

Nancy wasn't sure where to go with this. "Have you tried telling anyone...what you told me?"

"Nobody listens. Not even Mu-Ray."

"Will, you know your parents still—"

"Only Geoffrey listened, and Mau-ray took him away."

Nancy leaned down and rubbed the hair from the child's face. He sucked in hard to catch his breath. "Three minutes," he said.

"What happens in three minutes, Will?"

"He told me to count the seconds."

"Who told—?"

"Mori. He dared Geoffrey to hold his breath under water for three minutes. And he made me count, but Geoffrey lifted his head, so Mori pushed his head back under. And I counted, and he made it, but Mori said I counted too fast. I had to count real seconds. I had to start over, and if I didn't space out the count by seconds, I would have to start over again. I tried to keep the seconds, and Geoffrey fought. He pushed Geoffrey's head in further. One hundred twenty, one hundred twenty-one. And he fought harder. And then, I knew he would make it. One hundred sixty, one hundred sixty-one. I wanted to help Geoffrey fight, but Mori would make me start all over. And he's big and mean. One hundred seventy. We were so close, but then, he stopped fighting. Geoffrey stopped fighting. One hundred seventy-eight, one hundred seventy-nine, one eighty."

"Why had nobody ever met him, Will?"

"And when Mori let him go, Geoffrey floated down to the sandbar. Mori swole his arm in my face and said, 'Tell them I did it, friend.' And he walked away."

"There's nobody like that in the whole county, Will."

"I didn't even want to go down there," Will said. "Geoffrey said he really had something he wanted to show me. Like it used to be. Before…."

Will's tears took over his ambition to tell the story. Nancy realized that whatever Will thought he saw was his reality. His memory had solidified in the world he lived in now. This mystery person also resided in that world, and nothing could dissuade Will. At least not that night.

Again, she rubbed his head and used her sleeve to wipe away his tears. "Tomorrow," she said, "or whenever your dad gets home—"

"I can't tell them. No one believes me, never has. I could only talk to Geoffrey. Ever. And Mori took him away."

"It's Ok, Will. You're still—"

"And now, I talk to you, but he's on his way."

Nancy pushed Will away and stepped back toward the middle of the room.

"Will, that's not nice. Will!"

"I want...," Will began. "I want to go to bed."

"I'd say that's a good idea," Nancy said.

Nancy helped Will to his room. He was fragile, like when he was a baby, and she would carry him to bed. She'd wish him sweet dreams, but now he was, himself, a nightmare. Nancy understood how Will's mother must have felt all the time. He had been such a sweet boy with a good heart. Now, he would probably be sent to an institution as soon as his parents had time to transition from the birth of their miracle to the death that no one talked about. Nancy just wished she could lock the boy's door on the outside.

How do his parents even sleep in the house? she thought. When she returned downstairs, she decided to make coffee. She didn't normally drink coffee. In fact, if she had to make coffee at her own house, she would have no idea where to find anything. But she had made coffee for Mr. Crowe several times after she slept over after keeping Will late. He and Mrs. Crowe paid well, especially for poor farmers. Nancy always wanted to find a way to show her appreciation. Still, she definitely wasn't planning to take that money that was sitting on the table.

Then, she heard the voice in the sitting room.

"One hundred seventy-eight, one hundred seventy-nine, one hundred eighty."

Why is he back up? What is he doing? She tried to look into the room without actually going in, but she couldn't see the couch where the heard the counting continue.

She didn't want to pick up a knife and scare him. Would she really stab Will even to save her own life? She saw her purse still sitting on the counter. *Perfect!* The purse was small, but she grabbed it low near the opening. Heavy.

I could at least try to knock him back with the weight, she told herself, knowing the purse held everything she needed to protect herself.

"One hundred ninety-eight, one hundred ninety-nine...."

Nancy saw the money in his hand being counted. Then, she acknowledged that this grown, muscular man wasn't Will.

"...two hundred."

He was lying stretched out on the couch like her dad did, only he had the money rather than a drink.

"Where will I spend two hundred dollars in this little slice of heaven and remain invisible?" he asked.

"I'm calling the cops," Nancy said. "You better get out of here."

He laughed, said, "And you're telling the cops what? What that boy told you? Even he has learned that it's better sometimes just to make friends, stay friends, play nice. He knew I'd be friends with you. I knew you were coming over."

"You couldn't have. It was last minute."

"Your daddy knew."

The man watched the blood escape from Nancy's face.

"They'll believe Will now," Nancy said. "There's two of us."

The man laughed again. "Do you know that's exactly what that other boy said before I showed him a new game. He was actually pretty good at the game, but Will—he panicked. I just hate when people can't keep score right, you know what I mean?"

He sat up on the couch. Then, he leaned back, said, "But I want to play a different game with you, girl. I know you'd do just about anything to keep that little twerp safe up there."

Nancy walked around in front of the couch ad stood. She noticed the man's buzz cut, his blue jeans and tank top, and the clock tattoo on his left bicep that indicated 11:34. The words "*memento mori*" were etched under the clock.

"*Memento mori*," she said out loud.

"Yeah, baby, you know what that means?"

She shook her head.

"Always remember that you're going to die," he said, laughed, leaned back further. He opened his pants, said, "I think you know how to play this game."

She knelt in front of him, using the purse in her right hand to help guide herself down.

"Maybe you can earn some of this money back," he said, smiled, and tilted his head back, already a little satisfied just from the power.

"Memento mori," Nancy said.

"That's right, baby," he said, smiling.

As he reached down to help her please him, she reached into the purse and pulled out that .38 snub nose. The man known then as Mori felt the cold barrel underneath his stubbly chin, but he didn't feel it long enough to count even a real second.

THE END

189

The Figure

Emma Ingram

It sits looming in the corner of the second-hand shop. A small trinket of sorts. A faint whisper of mystery..if one was to listen in that particular direction. An easy glance over. A hidden surprise for fingers to softly lift from the ashes of forgotten things in the second-hand shop. The sharp corners, the strange tinges of red in the sun's glare. A small figure one could cup like a hot coffee, grasp like fine china. A figure, a silhouette. The other lost and forgotten things are silent, even the wind doesn't breath a gust here. You can feel it. In the air, a presence. A hand brushing across your spine. A women with a curse lurking in the shadows that we have grown to be wary of. Of what? Now that is a wise question.

*

Sam lounged with her feet on the dashboard. Dirty shoes making very dirty marks. To say this annoyed Jack wouldn't be a far stretch from reality. His eyes would make frequent calls to that dashboard, a ringing that wouldn't go away despite the voicemail option. Those eyes flicking back and forth, the way one might change the television channels. Sam remained as innocence as a new-born lamb, legs stumbling on shaky ground.

She twirled the object in her hand, glancing up at Jack, "Neat huh?"

Jack blinked, eyes moving from those dirty dirty marks to the figure she held.

"I mean, it's not my sorta thing but sure it's neat." He shrugged.

Sam looked at the small figure, jagged edges like the blade of a butcher's knife.

"Kinda freaky too," Turning it over she held it up to the window, "I could almost swear..."

Jack's eyebrows furrowed downwards, the lines of a book etching his forehead, "What?"

Sam lifted a shoulder half heartedly and bit her lip, "I could swear it has some kinda blood mark..."

Jack laughed. Chuckling as he glanced at Sam. They looked at each other with amused eyes. It was silly, they knew that. Of course they did. What they didn't realise, and would never come to realise, was that this was the last time they would ever meet with fond eyes and crinkling lips. Something made their car become a mangled mess of metal that very chilly morning. A sweet animal who didn't look twice when crossing the road? Oncoming traffic in the blind spot of all? A dark women with a dark request? Or perhaps a blood stained figure with ragged edges and a forgotten past.

*

Tony Lee Curtis put his foot to the metal, and the car lurched forward agreeably. The radio was blaring, voices ringing out. "Two young adults...car crash," Static interrupted the frequency, "Dead on impact." Tony gritted his teeth, a white knuckled grip on the leather steering wheel that he swung like a baseball bat. Squealing tires breaking the gravel into flying debris that spits on the glass. His car halted to a stop. In the silence Tony got out with small hesitant steps. The world was still, the only sound coming out of Tony was the hitches of breath as he gulped in what lay before his very feet. Two bodies, red ink painting the road and limbs twisted in unfamiliar angles. An elbow reaching for the lips of a girl. Knees worn like a basketball hat, backwards. Bodies like blow up dolls, abused, torn, thrown into the darkness by the harsh world we call home. Tony reached the nearest bush, and vomited up his, not so yummy looking now, turkey wrap. His wife had gone a great length to whip up that meal that chilly morning. She too would grow to understand that sometimes things don't happen as intended. Tony stood with shaking hands and a shaking mind. He glanced with a breath of gratitude, he was first on the scene. The mess he made could have been any other poor bastard. He brushed his stained lips of the cuff of his sleeve. Out of the corner of his eye sat a small black shadow, created by the figure that loomed above it. Tony reached down. Hand curling around it like a knot. A strange sensation overwhelmed him, circling around his body with sharp needles that pricked his skin. He heard car sirens growing closer in the distance. The knot increased, the sirens screamed in his ear. The sand had run empty in the hourglass. A force, perhaps created by man or perhaps something more sinister, slammed into Tony. His body was unrecognisable. The knot was tied, and a dead man was hanging. If only he hadn't grasp that figure, if only he had known.

*

The old man, withered and fading like the seasons changing, lay wheezing in his deathbed. Nothing surrounding him except absent memories, stale air, and a sense of satisfaction. His hand reached out and brushed the dark figure on his bed side table. It had come home to him. His mind wandered, remembering lost pieces to a puzzle unsolved. He saw an old women, much like himself now, cursing him with spit and venom. Vile words like that of a bullet, hitting him with an unnatural wall of power. He remembered throwing away the figure she had handed him. Not sparing a single thought until the stories soon crept through the thin walls. They floated through cracks and closed doors, through whispers and hushed voices. He had followed these stories, about the horror that followed the figure like a dark storm. With lightening like quick fire, your death was you're history. But he was always seconds too late, for the figure had crossed lakes and oceans leaving its blood stained footsteps in the mud. He was old, but not a fool. He understood that he could never atone for this simple mistake, for cheating the grim reaper with a careless wave of his arm. But as his head reached the soft creases of the pillow he held the figure, and surrendered. Death took him in his sleep. Peaceful, and soft with delicate fingers and gentle arms.

THE END

Published by VAX Books

VaxbookZ.com

Printed in Great Britain
by Amazon